Avenue Of Madness

A murder mystery that takes place
on Madison Avenue in the 1960's

Bob Schmalenberger

authorHOUSE®

AuthorHouse™
1663 Liberty Drive
Bloomington, IN 47403
www.authorhouse.com
Phone: 1-800-839-8640

First published by AuthorHouse 07/18/2011

ISBN: 978-1-4634-1725-3 (ebk)
ISBN: 978-1-4634-1726-0 (hc)
ISBN: 978-1-4634-1727-7 (sc)

Library of Congress Control Number: 2011909775

Printed in the United States of America

Cover design and illustration by Bob Schmalenberger

This book is dedicated to my loving wife Joyce whose love, loyalty and infinite wisdom, continues to inspire me. Thank you, Joyce.

Table of Contents

Preface

How did this happen?

I'm totally bewildered.

I'm standing over the body of the man I hate most in the world, and I didn't kill him.

My mind is desperately trying to escape from this situation and is uncontrollably jumping around over the events of the last 10 years that have brought me to be here at this place in time. Most of the flashing images involve the victim, but many are just a sordid, jumbled collection of disturbing things I have experienced in this, sometimes, insane business of advertising and before. The first thought that pops into my head is what Sigmund Freud said, "*The goal of all life is death.*"

— Robert Randall – March 23, 1965

The beginning

The first image that comes zooming into my head is my mother's cheerful, smiling face looking down at me as she did every morning when I was growing up.

"Robert, get up, you've got to get to school."

"Aw mom just a few minutes more."

I roll over but she pulls the covers off me.

"You'll miss the bus, Robert, hurry up get up."

She's a great mom. She loves telling me the story of how, after I was born in Brooklyn, New York, she brought me home from the hospital in the middle of a gigantic blizzard to where they lived at the time in Maspeth, Queens. "The car was sliding all over the road, I didn't think we were going to make it." She would relish telling me.

As the full image takes form, I realize it's around 1948, the time I'm going to P.S. 147, in a little town called Cambria Heights, a humble New York City suburb in Queens, where we lived. Ever since I was a little kid the name of our community itself has always brought forth in my mind images of a regal country town in the north of England, overlooking lush rolling hills dotted with cottages sporting thick thatched roofs. It's actually located on the edge of the City alongside the "Belt Parkway," the new highway that wraps itself around the girth of Brooklyn and Queens, separating the City from Nassau County like a huge, asphalt "belt." This area was originally dozens of square miles of vegetable "truck farms" that the real estate developers gobbled-up and packed with thousands of tiny homes right after World War II, each crammed on it's own postage stamp sized lot. The term "truck farm," came from the fact that most of the vegetables grown there were bought by local entrepreneurs who loaded them onto trucks and hawked them on the streets in the surrounding neighborhoods. "Fresh vegetables, fresh fruit. Get your fresh fruit and vegetables, right here," the drivers would shout as they slowly drove up and down the streets, stopping occasionally to give the housewives a chance to buy. It was a very good seasonal business.

But to me, Cambria Heights is heaven, a congenial loving place to grow up, a blue-collar community where all the families actually get along because they have so much in common.

"Get up, Robert," she repeats, "you know if your father was here, you'd be up and dressed and on your way."

My "Pop" is a New York City fireman and has to work three days at a time, a shift called a "72," so he's not always around to get us up. My older brother Jack is an enterprising guy; he is up at 4 a.m., driving his way around Queens in a bread truck, delivering bread and pastry to bakeries and food stores. Despite the fact that Jack is only 15 he has somehow gotten a driver's license, a testament to his enterprising spirit. He's a big guy and looks 20. My younger brother Don is already downstairs in the cellar feeding his collection of snakes. He and his friend, Walter Mulroney, want to be herpetologists. I remember Don once exhibited his collection of snakes at Brooklyn Technical High School. Of the dozens of exhibits there, his was the most crowded. You couldn't even get into the classroom where he was performing. It was like a sideshow at the circus. He is such a wonderful showman.

The vision of Jack the year before comes into my mind. He's a delivery-boy for "Abe the butcher" in the meat market up on Linden Boulevard. He had to peddle that crazy looking delivery bike with the small front tire and the huge front basket designed for carrying hundreds of pounds of meat to homes all over Cambria Heights.

Now I'm picturing him going to pick up some window signs for Abe at a sign shop in Jamaica, Queens. While he is there he persuades the owner, Seymour Fishman, to give me a job as a delivery boy. I think he was mostly motivated by the thought of his not having to waste any more of his valuable time picking up signs in Jamaica. If he wasn't delivering meat, he wasn't getting any tips, and tips were paramount to him. He knew how to charm the ladies into giving him big tips. He'd carry the bundles into their kitchens and even offer to pack their refrigerators for them.

"You really should have a delivery-boy and my brother, Bob, would be perfect for you and he even has some drawing ability," Jack said he told Seymour.

"Have him come in and see me."

Two days later, I go in and meet Seymour and start delivering signs for him. I'm only 12-years old and still in grammar school, but I'm the tallest kid in the class and look 18. In the years that follow, Seymour not only teaches me how to do sign lettering, he teaches me about art, business and life. He introduced me to the philosophers. He told me to look up *"The Inner Man"* by Plato: *"Beauty depends on simplicity — I mean the true simplicity of a rightly and nobly ordered mind and character. He is a fool who seriously inclines to weigh the beautiful by any other standard than that of the good. The good is the beautiful. Grant me to be beautiful in the inner man."* I have strived for that all my life.

That fateful event eventually turned me into a pretty darn-good lettering artist.

I'm reminded that my brother Jack was really responsible for pointing me in the direction that shaped my whole life. Thank you, Jack.

The 3-year journey from 23rd Street to Madison Avenue

Suddenly the scene shifts to 1957 and I'm holding a bright piece of parchment paper in my hand with the image of Albrecht Dürer in a blue circle in the top left hand corner. The name of the art school is printed across the top of the document. My name is hand written across the center in beautiful calligraphy with the word "Honor" hand-lettered below it. It's my diploma from the New York School of Art & Design. The art history teacher of the school, Harry Connolly, had chosen Dürer to be the guiding image for the school, not only due to his outstanding drawing and painting skills, but his pioneering graphic wood block and printmaking abilities, all pre-cursers to the advertising industry.

Thanks in part to my brother Jack's pushiness, I had won a full scholarship to the school 3-years earlier because my lettering ability, that I learned from Seymour Fishman, so impressed the faculty at the school that they had given me a full scholarship.

"Hi, Robert, how are you doing?"

It's Marcia Schwartz one of the students I went to art school with, she comes walking into the main classroom from the lobby. The school is located on 23rd Street in Manhattan in the top floor penthouse of the Flatiron Building, the city's first skyscraper, built back in 1902.

Marcia had just graduated and had gotten a job at DDBO the big advertising agency located up on the infamous Madison Avenue.

"Great, Marcia, I made it." I hold up my diploma pointing to the big word "Honor" in the lower left.

"Yes, I know, congratulations."

Martin Mayer says in his famous book, "Madison Avenue, U.S.A.," that, "Madison Avenue is the only major street in New York City named after a U.S. President." He also says the ad guys refer to it as "Ad Alley," or more appropriately, "Ulcer Gulch." It's a mere 6-miles long but is responsible for the sale of more antacids and alcohol than any other street in the world. I spend the 4-hours that I commute everyday back and forth from school reading every book I can find on the advertising business.

"Robert, they are looking for an assistant art director at DDBO. I told them your lettering skills would be perfect for the job."

Marcia always was a bit of a pushy broad in art school, so it is no surprise that she did some bragging to one of the art directors at DDBO about my ability to do lettering. Fortunately, the art director works on one of their largest accounts, Phillips Appliances, which she says needs an assistant art director who can letter with speed and accuracy.

"They do tons of full-page ads in newspapers across the country, all loaded with lots of headlines sub-headlines copy and pictures of their appliances. And the client wants to see them all before he approves an ad."

At this point my mind jumps to the interview for the job.

"Hello, Bob is it?"

"Yes, Bob Randall."

"Nice to meet you Bob, I'm Jack Stein."

He's seated behind a drawing board with his back to the window, which overlooks Madison Avenue. He has an unusually odd habit of twisting his head from side to side as he speaks. It appears to be a nervous tick.

"Thank you, I'm glad to be here."

"Marcia tells me your pretty good at lettering."

"I've worked in a sign shop for the past 8-years."

"Okay, what typeface is this?" He says, spinning around in his swivel chair and pointing to a type chart on the wall behind him.

"Franklin Gothic."

"And, this?"

"Baskerville."

"What about this one."

"Times Roman."

"This one?"

"Caslon-540."

"Here," he hands me a sheet of yellow copywriter's paper that has headlines, sub-heads, copy, lists of appliances and prices typed on it.

"Go sit down at that drawing table out there, Bob, and do a comp layout of this full-page ad, here are the photos of all the appliances," he points to a drawing table outside his office.

I sit down, feeling immediately at home and knock out the layout in less than 20-minutes.

"Done." I proclaim proudly, rushing into Jack's office and handing him the finished layout.

"That was fast. Damn good job, Bob."

"Thank you." I smiled.

He escorts me back to the drawing table.

"You're now my new Assistant Art Director, put your coat in that closet over there and sit here, this is now your drawing board and taboret from now on."

"Taboret?"

"That's a fancy French word for an art storage table."

The ad I did, went over to the client that afternoon.

Even the client was impressed with the job I did.

My mind jumps to another morning, I'm up at 5 a.m. to make my usual trip to the City; the "Q-4" bus from Cambria Heights to Jamaica and the "F" subway train to Manhattan. Only on this morning I'm not going to art school at the Flatiron Building, I'm going to 47th Street to work at DDBO. On this day I'm too excited to finish reading Martin Mayer's book.

DDBO Advertising is one of the largest, most famous, advertising agencies in the world. It's located on Madison Avenue in mid-town Manhattan. It was named for the 4 founders: Alvin Dudley of New York City, Harold Davis of Buffalo, New York, Philip Billings, of Chicago, and Arthur Olsen of Boston: "Dudley, Davis, Billings & Olsen." But it's not cool to ever say the individual names, just "DDBO." They actually have a handbook that tells exactly how to say the name. It is never proper to include the "&."

More recent images of the past 10-years at DDBO begin to race through my mind lickety-split, like the spinning cylinder that Edward Muybridge used to prove that at some point a horse does have all four feet off the ground at the same time when it is running. He not only settled a bet, it led to the discovery of motion pictures.

It's been an exciting ride, from Assistant Art Director to Art Director to Art Group-Head to Head Art Director and finally Creative Director of the Boston office. I have been fortunate enough to create ads for some of the most prestigious companies and products in America; beer, cosmetics, hotels, cars, fabrics, children's clothes, computers, soup – dozens altogether.

The New York School of Art & Design prepared me very well for what I have to face everyday in this insanely fast-paced world of advertising. When I started, not only did I have to hit the ground running, the ground was moving at a hundred miles an hour. Although I didn't truly appreciate it at the time, I'm glad that the school placed so much emphasis on meeting deadlines, and coming up with new ideas and executing them quickly. I also learned to change direction if the client wanted me to. The advertising business is nothing but speed. I am very grateful for all the added confidence that The New York School of Art & Design instilled in me. It gives me a big advantage over other DDBO art department employees.

It's so ironic, my lettering expertise along with my drawing skills and the knowledge and self-confidence Seymour had instilled in me not only got me the scholarship they got me my job at DDBO just two-dozen blocks north of the art school on 23rd Street.

Here at DDBO, I came to learn that "The Client is King" and everything humanly possible is done to satisfy them. Some of the things I, a green naive kid from Cambria Heights witnessed, are unbelievably bizarre; like my first encounter with Tom James, which begins to take shape in my mind.

My first encounter with Tom James

I flash back to my office at the agency in New York. I hear the voice of Steve Svenson, head art director of the New York office, come projecting ahead of him as he bursts into my office, the look of mortal fear contorts his usually calm Swedish face. He's a quiet, likable guy who the older copywriters call "Sven."

"Can you stay late tonight, Bob?"

He doesn't wait for my answer, he knows what it will be, he always knows.

"Get over to Tom James' office right away, he'll fill you in on what you have to do."

"Okay, but Steve I've got to finish this tune-in ad for Global Broadcasting, it has to be at the newspaper by seven tonight, and it's almost six o'clock now."

"Please go over and see Tom James, first." Steve is now almost pleading with me.

The whole agency knows Steve Svenson is nearing retirement and he is deathly afraid he's not going to make it. Some of the senior art directors told me he used to be a happy-go-lucky guy who always had a smile on his face and a twinkle in his eye. But lately the stress of not reaching his impending retirement has turned him into a demon.

"Hurry, Bob, Tom's waiting."

I've come to find out, Tom James is one of the "Young Turks," as they call themselves, a group of new guys who are vowed and determined to overthrow the current regime in power at DDBO, and take over the agency. I've heard a lot about Tom, all bad, but I haven't worked with him, yet.

If Steve doesn't make it to retirement age, and get "fully-vested," he'll lose a huge chunk of money. It's one of the famous tricks of the advertising business, "always keeping the mice chasing after the cheese," right to the end. Last month one of the top account supervisors was less than a year from being fully vested when they canned him. His retirement money was forfeited and divided among all of the remaining top executives in their retirement accounts. Sven is a good man, but he's running scared and burning out.

"Get going, Bob, please!"

I jump up, grab a layout pad some charcoal pencils and start a fast trot down the hall toward the other side of the building where the copywriters are located.

"Thanks Bob, I really, really, appreciate this." His Swedish accent follows me down the hall.

I round the bank of elevators that service the art department on this side of the building and zip past the opposite bank into the copy department.

The stories of how Tom James has ruthlessly fought his way to one of the two corner offices in the copy department are legendary. The advertising business has a strange turf feudal system, you first start work at the dingy center core of building and fight your way through the "bull-pens" and partitioned offices until you finally succeed in getting to the light; an outside office with a window. But, you're not done yet, you then have to claw your way to a corner office, being measured and judged every agonizing move of the way.

I head to the southwest corner of the building where Tom James' corner office is located overlooking Vanderbuilt Avenue and 46th Street.

As I approach, I see his overweight secretary, Mildred, sitting at her desk outside his office munching on some of her favorite cookies. She has a couple in her mouth and her hand disappearing out of sight into the biggest, brightest, yellow box of "Mallomars" that I have ever seen. I've never seen a box that large.

She sees me, "Mumm, watch out he's in a shitty mood."

"Thanks for the warning."

"Tom, Robert Randall is here."

Tom James spots me, "Get your ass in here, Randall."

I maneuver past his desk and sit in one of the huge, maroon wingback chairs in front of his desk.

"Randall, wait 'til I'm done with this copy."

I sit back and watch him, as he pecks away on his old Royal typewriter, one-finger-at-a-time.

"Clack, clack, clack..."

Although he has the appearance of being a tall man, he actually has a stubby body, so he looks short when he is sitting down. His face is gaunt with deep groves chiseled in each cheek. His hair is jet-black and his dark brown beady eyes always appear to be trying to pierce into your psyche. I think he's about 5-years older than me although he looks more than 10-years older. I'm told he always wears a black suit. They say he must have a dozen and he never takes off his jacket. Never.

For some reason he is constantly popping some kind of pill. No one knows if it's some kind of candy for energy or medicine for a mysterious illness. His brown-nosing subordinates say its candy while his legions of enemies say it is drugs. Nobody really knows for sure. And, I don't think they really care. I just can't help but wonder what makes a man like this tick.

Life around Tom James is only about survival. Everyone develops their own style of dealing with him, to come away with as few wounds as possible after each skirmish.

He looks up from his typewriter, "The Norman Cosmetics account is in trouble, Randall, you need to lay out these five shade-promotion ads tonight. Hal Norman expects them to be on his desk when he sits down at it, at seven in the morning."

I've learned that a shade-promotion ad is one for a specific shade of nail polish and lipstick combined. In this case Norman Cosmetics' newest shade, "Moon Glow."

"Where's the copy?"

"Right here."

He throws five sheets of yellow paper at me, I catch 3 but 2 of them flutter down to the floor.

"Pick those up, you asshole."

I quickly swoop down sweep them up and slump back into the chair to read the copy.

"Now, here's what I want; the first one has a sexy broad in an evening gown standing on the edge of a cliff in the moonlight with a guy down on the beach. Make the guy look like Burt Lancaster. The headline is, 'Moon Glow will brighten your life and bring love beaming in.'" "Don't forget to draw her with big tits, Hal Norman likes models with big tits."

I open my layout pad and rapidly sketch out the size of the ad; a spread in "Life Magazine."

"And don't forget to stick the Moon Glow lipstick and nail polish down in the right corner with the logo. In the other ads have broads with big tits in different locations with the guys sniffing around somewhere nearby. And don't forget to put a moon in the picture."

"Who's going to bring the layouts up to the client after I have them done?"

"Mildred, get Phil Tucker up here, now," he yells to Mildred, who's now probably wondering how late she's going home tonight.

"I won't have them done 'til after midnight, Tom," he ignores me.

"The other headlines are just as great, make them all readable, Randall. Show me a quick sketch of what the layouts are going to look like, hurry up."

I rough out the first ad, placing the model in the upper left hand corner with the moon in the upper right and the headline in between. I put the man on the rocks below, climbing up toward the model, thinking about where I'm going to find a photo of Burt Lancaster to use as reference.

"That's good, Randall, I want them all to be the best God damned layouts you have ever done, or you'll be looking for a new job. Now get your ass out of my office and get to work."

I start to leave as Phil Tucker, the Norman Cosmetics account executive enters the office, puffing.

"Tucker, you're going to take the fucking layouts, that Randall's doing tonight, up to Hal Norman's office first thing in the morning, they have to be on his desk before 7 a.m."

"But..."

"There are no buts, Tucker. Randall, you call him when they're done. Got it?"

"Got it. Give me your home number, Phil."

Tom stops walking to his desk and spins his head around, "Home? He's not going home. Tucker, I want you to put together a complete print media plan for these ads for the rest of the year. And, don't even think about leaving until it's done."

Phil writes his extension number on the top of one of the yellow copy papers. "Call me when they're done, Bob."

"Okay, I've got to get going, I still have to finish an ad for Global Broadcasting."

"Fuck the ad for Global Broadcasting you finish my ads first or you're a dead man, Randall. You'll be looking for a new job, tonight."

"Okay," I don't argue, I know I will somehow have to get the Global tune-in ad done first.

"You remember Randall; you're either with me or against me." Tom hits me with the same threat that I've heard he uses on everyone.

I don't say a word; I sense it's useless to question the decisions of a mad man.

My first encounter with Tom James leaves me with a strong foreboding feeling about my future at DDBO. It reminds me of something amusing that Sigmund Freud once said, *"The first man to use abusive language instead of his fists was the founder of civilization."*

Total humiliation

My mind now jumps to Boston and to another experience with Tom James.

"Randall, get your ass over here, right away," the voice on the other end of the phone screams. I know instantly it's Tom James. I feel a sudden clenching in the pit of my stomach. The clenching that they told me about when I first joined the agency that I would eventually feel anytime I worked with Tom James.

"Where are you, Tom?"

"I'm at Dream Shampoo, get over here right away, I want you to do some layout changes for me."

The headquarters of Dream Shampoo is located across town in South Boston.

"Now, I want you here, now!"

I know the layouts were done in the New York office because he never let's us touch the creative for Dream Shampoo. He considers us the poor out-of-town stepchildren when it comes to creative ideas. Besides he doesn't want the client to even think about having us do the creative here in the Boston office. That would totally diminish his power.

"I'll send over Hal Pearson."

"No, you asshole, I want you over here, now," Tom bellows.

"Okay, I'm on my way."

"Don't forget to bring your layout pad, markers and rubber cement," he adds, as he abruptly hangs up.

When I get to the lobby of the Dream Shampoo Company on the south side of the city, Bill Johnson, one of the associate creative directors in the New York office, meets me.

"He's even more crazy than usual," Bill whispers, as he ushers me into the Dream Shampoo boardroom.

"Get over here, Randall," Tom James' yell echo's.

"See this layout? I want you to change the headline."

He hands me a piece of paper that he has scribbled the new headline on.

"Tom, I can't read the first part."

"'Feel like a million, look like a billion, with Dream Shampoo,' you idiot."

I immediately begin to letter the headline onto the bond paper layout pad that I will use to make a patch to go over the existing headline on the New York art department layout.

As I get the first three words lettered he screams, "No, stop!"

I stop.

"Make it: 'Feel like a billion, look like a million, with Dream Shampoo.'"

I tear off the page and start again, after I letter another three words, he yells: "No, no, stop, make it: 'Feel like a million, look like a billion, with Dream Shampoo.'"

"Make up your mind, Tom," Bill Johnson says, "the client will be back in ten minutes."

"That's it, do it, Randall."

I finish the headline, cut it out and use the rubber cement I brought to paste it over the headline in the layout.

"Good, now get the hell out of here and wait in the lobby in case I need you again."

About an hour goes by, Tom and Bill come storming out of the boardroom with serious looks on their faces.

"Let's go," Tom says, motioning like a military leader for all of us to leave. He likes to pretend he's a general, even though he has never been in the army. He even tries to march like George S. Patton, with an exaggerated motion, swinging his arms with his fists clenched, while he takes giant strides. It's comical.

Out on the street in front of the building we head to the train station, Tom is afraid of flying so he takes the train; he only visits the Boston clients. He's never been to any of the other clients in the rest of the country.

"Watch this, Randall, you want to see how much Bill Johnson owes me?"

He takes the giant, black leather portfolio loaded with a dozen large layouts and throws it at Bill Johnson, hitting him squarely in the stomach knocking the air out of him and sending him sprawling on the ground, tearing a hole in the left knee of his pants.

"Get up and carry it, Johnson, you peasant."

Johnson just sits on the ground, holding his stomach.

"That's how much he owes me, Randall. He's nothing without me."

"I made him what he is today, an Associate Creative Director, I got him onto the board, I got him the big office next to mine. I did it all,

I'm Tom James, and I can treat people anyway I want." Tom shouts, while shaking his fist at the Dream Shampoo building.

"What happened in there, Bill?"

"It's better if you don't know." Bill struggles to get to his feet, motioning for us to get going.

"Get up Johnson and let's get the fuck out of this second rate city."

Freud said, *"A neurosis is the result of a conflict between the ego and the id; the person is at war with himself. A psychosis is the outcome of a similar disturbance in the relation between the ego and the outside world."*

With Tom James, I think it's both.

Peeping Ralph

Now I see myself in the New York office once again. It's after midnight; I'm walking to the other side of the building to the copy department. The long banks of fluorescent lights that hang over the dozens of tiny cubicles that house the agency's copywriting staff are all dark. The cleaning crew has turned them off after they finished emptying the trash baskets, hours ago. There is a faint glow coming from the window offices at the far side of the copy department along 46th Street. I'm delivering a half a dozen layouts to one the copy supervisors, Vincent Glenn, whose office is located on the outside wall of the building. He had given me the headlines and copy at five o'clock to put into layout form for him to present to the client in the morning. The client is Italy's government owned airline, "Air Italy," and the layouts are for the introduction of the airline's new jets that will be zipping people "over-the-pond" to Rome in record time. It is a secret project and I'm working on it at night so no one else in the creative department will know about the upcoming announcement of the jets. The airline business is a cutthroat business and if the information were to leak out it would be disastrous for the airline and the agency. I walk slowly; the layouts under my left arm and my right hand feeling along the glass topped partitions. I know them all by heart even in the dark I have made this trip so many times every day. As I pass Bill Jones' cubicle, Phil Mancuso's cubicle, Roberta

Ellison's cubicle, I tick them off in my mind on my way to Vincent Glenn's office. I briefly pause at Roberta's tiny office for a minute. She's the sister of the president of one of the agency's largest clients: "New York Utilities." She's so rich she never cashes her paychecks, she just puts them in her bottom desk drawer and periodically one of the women from the payroll department comes up to collect them and deposit them in her account.

I arrive at the cubicle outside Vincent Glenn's office where his secretary, Mary, sits in the daytime. The glow coming from the offices on each side is now intensified. The door to Vincent's office is closed. I feel for the handle and open it. He said that he would leave it unlocked for me. I move toward his desk to place the layouts in the center so he won't miss them in the morning. As I glide them to a gentle landing on his desk calendar mat, his chair suddenly begins to turn slowly around. My heart starts to beat faster; fear sends a rippling chill over my entire body. I jump back hitting the table and chair by the wall behind me, falling to the floor. A silhouette of a man rises out of the chair and a voice says: "Can I help you?"

I stutter: "Who are you? What are you doing here?"

The figure is now standing up fully and begins to walk toward me. I'm panicked and start to breathe hard. His silhouette is now looming over me on the floor, clearly outlined in the eerie light. He looks like he is a tall, skinny man with bushy hair and a big bulge is outlined in the right hand pocket of his suit jacket.

Could he be some business spy who is here to steal the Air Italy layouts, or is he a murderer?

"Sorry to scare you, here let me help you up," the silhouette says, as it reaches down and helps me to my feet.

It is now that I see from the glow that it is Ralph Hill the head of the print production department.

The whole agency knows that every night from around eleven o'clock on, after everyone has gone home and all the lights are turned out in the copy department, one figure prowls the halls and private window offices of the DDBO copy department. It's Ralph with his giant pair of binoculars swinging in his jacket pocket. He slithers in and out of all the window offices spying on the Roosevelt Hotel across the street hoping to see some couple engaged in sex. I'm told he has even made a deal with the desk clerk to put the hookers and pretty women in those rooms on this side of the hotel on the same floor as this floor of the agency's copy department. He sits there for hours sometimes running up and down the hall every time he sees the lights going on in one of the hotel rooms. This is the first time I've run into him at night. In the daytime he always looks like an unmade bed, with disheveled gray hair and the shoulders of his wrinkled, dark blue pin-stripe suit piled with drifts of unusually large titanium white flakes of dandruff.

"You scared the shit out of me, Ralph," I yell, too embarrassed to admit I should have guessed immediately that it was him.

"Sorry, Bob, sorry, I didn't mean to frighten you," he responds sheepishly, "I'm out-a here."

"I never expected to find you in here, the door was closed," is all I can muster as my excuse.

He sneaks out of the office and disappears in the dark of the hallway.

"See-ya tomorrow, Bob."

As I straighten the table, I glance over to the hotel and see there is a couple involved in sex on the bed in one of their sleazy rooms. That was what he was watching.

I turn back to the pile of layouts; give them a fast twist to make sure they are sitting perfectly straight on Vincent's desk. I roll his chair up to his desk and quickly walk to the door twist the lock in the doorknob, as I was instructed, and pull the door closed behind me.

Vincent will be all set for the meeting and Al won't be able to get back into the office. No one will be able to get back into the office except Vincent in the morning.

Once again, I use the Braille system to make my way back to my office still breathing hard from my scary red-faced experience.

A little gray hair

"Get in here, Randall," Tom James voice pops into my head, booming from his office in his standard rude tone, pointing to the large wingback chair in front of his desk.

"Sit down."

I enter and proceed to sit as ordered.

Tom bolts past me with a piece of his yellow copy paper in his hand, "Here, Mildred type this right away. And none of your usual mistakes."

He is always in a big hurry, actually running the few steps to his secretary's desk to get his precious copy typed. He wants everyone to believe everything he is doing is more important than anything anyone else is doing, even if it isn't.

As he rounds the chair I'm now sitting in, on his way to his desk, he abruptly stops behind the chair.

"You're getting gray, Randall." His tone is almost jubilant.

I wonder, what kind of person takes even a second out of his busy day to comment on his underling's hair. It seems more like something a woman would be apt to mention to another woman, not a man to another man, especially two men who work together. You're a strange one Tom James. What makes you tick? What is there in your upbringing and background that has you worrying about another man's hair turning gray? My father was gray before he was 40, so it isn't a big surprise that I am getting a few gray hairs already. I had never even noticed it. Who or what in his life preloaded him with the need to demean everyone to make himself feel superior? He seems to relish it even more when he does it in front of a large group, as if he's sending a message to all of them, also. I've come to realize that it's all part of the regular psychiatric dueling he is always engaging in, with me and others.

Freud said: *"The fateful question of the human species seems to be whether and to what extent the cultural process developed in it will succeed in mastering the derangements of communal life caused by the human instinct of aggression and self-destruction. Men have brought their powers of subduing the forces of nature to such a pitch that by using them they could now very easily exterminate one another to the last man."*

"Okay, 'Old man' Randall, let's see those layouts."

What a little man, its no wonder everyone wants to see him dead.

An outing at the DDBO Company Outing

Now, the early morning June daylight casts long shadows across the highway as Dom Martinetti and I share a ride to the Company's annual outing. Dom is another art director at the agency. He lives out near where I live and we sometimes commute to the office together. He is older and has a family.

Every spring the agency takes all the male employees on an outing to the Westchester Country Club up in exclusive Westchester County. The female employees are not invited, only the men. The women have to stay back at the office to answer the phones. Most of the high-level female executives spend the day sulking and plotting retaliation, infuriated at being treated like inferior human beings.

As Dom turns up into the driveway to the clubhouse, we see a lot of familiar faces running around on the ball fields on either side of the road, involved in several games of softball.

We get to the parking lot and find a spot way at the back. I grab my swimming bag from the back seat and Dom and I casually stroll around to size-up the place.

We're both from lower middle-class families and this is the first country club we've ever been to. Most of the account executives and the top brass of the agency are off playing golf, the real reason the company outing was created in the first place. We all get a chance to come along so they can play golf. As we continue our reconnoitering I notice there are a few dozen of the younger account guys over at the tennis courts. We pass them as we head over to the swimming pool area.

"Bob, you and Dom want to play some tennis with us?"

"No thanks, Charlie, I'm headed to the indoor swimming pool." I've never played tennis I don't even own a tennis racket.

As we continue, we see there are two huge, bright blue, outdoor pools surrounded by hundreds of lounge chairs. There are some women members and their screaming kids casually enjoying the pool and their cocktails as they must do everyday while their husbands are in the hot city making the money to keep up their memberships. Near one of the pool entrances are several very attractive women members in bikinis. They are laughing and flaunting themselves on the deck chairs despite the fact that I don't think any of them are even supposed to be here today, because the Club has been taken over exclusively by the agency for the whole day. It appears that these women are definitely here to play games and have fun taunting all the advertising men with their skimpy bathing suits.

"Let's go and see what's inside, Dom, I want to find the indoor pool," I gesture toward the gigantic Clubhouse.

"Alright, sounds like a perfectly good idea to me," he responds in his usual muted, laid-back tone.

We climb the wide granite staircase to the dark walnut doors at the main entrance.

Inside, the lobby walls are dark, framed with crown-molding walnut panels. There are dozens of plush chairs clustered in small groups around the spacious lobby area.

Off to the left are two separate rooms, one is the bar and the other is the main dining room. The bar is the biggest I've ever seen, it must be over 150-feet long with a crew of a half-dozen energetic bartenders, mixing, shaking and delivering legions of the preferred drink of Madison Avenue, tall-stemmed gin martinis, to the parched throngs of DDBOers swarming around the bar. The room is cram-packed with dozens of agency guys laughing yelling and having an all-round good time. They are dressed in casual clothes; it's really weird that there is not a Brooks Brothers suit among them.

Dom and I find an open spot at the far end of the bar. The bartender asks me what I want.

"A glass of milk."

"A glass of milk? Are you kidding?" is his laughing retort.

"This guy wants a glass of milk," he yells to the other bartenders.

"We don't have any milk, kid, this is a man's bar," one of the older bartenders shouts back from the other end of the bar.

"Get him a glass of milk," a loud, authoritative voice comes booming from the opposite end of the bar.

It's Steve Svenson, my boss. He's clearly a very popular guy, looking like the stereotypical Swede that could have been sent over from the agency's casting department.

An embarrassed look appears on the face of the older loud-mouthed bartender as he turns and orders one of the younger bartenders to go to the kitchen and "get me a glass of milk, fast."

Within a minute a large glass of milk arrives being carried high on a serving tray by the now red-faced younger bar keep.

I grab the glass from the moving tray, turn to Steve Swenson, lift it high in the air and toast him.

"Thank you, Steve."

"You're more than welcome, Bob."

At this point, the entire room bursts into a round of applause and cheering.

I'm a little embarrassed, but definitely feel vindicated.

After a quick lunch I tell Dom I'm going to look for the indoor pool. It's bound to be quieter than those outdoor pools without the women members and the kids to contend with.

"Okay, I'll see you later, Bob, maybe we can see if we can get into one of those softball games after you've had your swim."

"Sounds good, to me."

I follow the signs to the men's locker room.

It's very fancy with the same dark paneling as the lobby on not only the walls but the lockers too and there's thick dark putting green looking carpet on the floor.

"Where is the pool?" I ask the attendant at the door.

"Through there," he gestures to a set of doors at the end of the locker room, "You can use any of these lockers on this side of the room."

I quickly change into my bathing suit and head for the pool.

"There are towels in the pool area," the attendant calls after me as I push through one of the two fancy swinging doors into the pool.

The pool is styled after a Roman bath with marble everywhere. There are enormous skylights over the entire natatorium and comfortable bleacher seats along the far wall. A lot classier than the pool at the New York Athletic Club in Manhattan where I competed during the time that I was going to art school.

There's not a soul in the pool area, the pool is as smooth as glass not a ripple or blemish. I can see the bright blue sky reflecting off the surface from the skylights.

This is one of my favorite times to dive into a pool when it is absolutely still. I have set my best times in pools when they're like this because there is almost no resistance during the first lap and you get a back wave on the second lap that can chop seconds off the time.

I approach the edge of the pool and pause for a few seconds, take several deep breaths and spring forward in a standard pancake-style racing dive. The water is cold and invigorating as I break the surface and begin a long deliberate freestyle stroke toward the other end. I glide along smoothly touch the wall, do a flip turn, and head back. I wish someone were here timing me I think I just set my best record for the fifty-yard freestyle as I tap the wall.

I climb up the ornate ladder, get out of the pool and take two of the plush towels from the table near the door. They smell good with the fresh aroma of flowers.

I go over and flop into one of the dark walnut deck chairs carefully lined up along the wall on the marble floor and put the second towel around my neck.

It's so peaceful I begin to relax.

Suddenly the door from the locker room swings open, in comes Jack Ryan one of the copywriters that I work with.

"Hi, Jack," I greet him.

"Hi, Bob, how's the water?"

"Chilly, but very refreshing."

As he comes up the stairs and fully in to view I'm shocked to see that he's not wearing a bathing suit.

And I also notice he is very handsomely endowed. My God it reaches halfway down to his knees.

"Jack, what are you doing, you don't have a bathing suit on?"

"I don't need a suit there are only men here today," he responds.

"Jack, I saw some female members out at the pool."

"They're not supposed to be here, this is a 'men's-only' outing, tough luck on them," is his smart-alec response.

"Well it's nice of you to give your 'Johnson' an outing of his own."

Just then the doors at the far end of the pool open and an official looking club man wearing a name tag comes in apparently showing the pool to two women who appear to be checking it out for a function their company is planning.

The man stops in his tracks. "You should have a bathing suit on," he indignantly shouts at Jack. He also has a distinct look of jealousy on his embarrassed face. Both the women are clearly impressed, snickering at each other.

Jack ignores him and dives into the water.

"Tell him to put on a bathing suit," the man says to me while Jack is under the water.

"I'm very sorry," the man says to the two women he is showing around.

He puts his arms on their shoulders, quickly spins them around to escort them out of the pool area.

"Tell him to put on a suit, or I will have him ejected from the club," he yells, as the swinging door closes behind him and Jack pops up out of the water.

"Is that asshole gone, yet? I couldn't hold my breath much longer."

Field of tears

After my not so relaxing swim experience, I hook up with Dom again in the bar. "Dom, do we want to see if we can play some softball?"

"Why of course Bob, why not, let's take a walk over to the ball fields."

"Dom, do you know Jack Ryan?"

"Yes, I do, I've worked with him he's a good writer."

We get up and head toward the lobby.

I smile.

"Why, Bob, have you seen Jack?"

"I'll say."

"Hey Randall, want another glass of milk?" One of the smart-ass junior account executives seated at the bar asks as we pass by.

"No thanks, sonny."

On the way down to the ball fields I give Dom a detailed report about Jack Ryan's performance.

"Jack just put on quite an impressive show at the indoor swimming pool."

"Is he a good swimmer?"

"No, he's a good swinger."

"Swinger?"

"He's hung like a bull elephant."

"He's what?"

"He came into the pool without a bathing suit."

"That's strange, why would he do that?"

"I think he just wanted to show off."

"Well, Bob, it sounds like he impressed you."

"He also impressed the two pretty women who were being given a tour of the facility."

"Oh."

"When the club executive tried to rush the women out of the pool, they kept turning around to get a better look at Jack's record-setting equipment, it was funny."

We stop to watch the ball game for a while expecting to see DDBO employees having a good time.

But instead, we see a lot of confused and angry guys.

Tom James is out on the mound, pitching.

It's unbelievable, he's crying, balling like a baby, apparently because his team is losing.

The annual tradition has the teams divided into two groups of DDBO employees; the copywriters against the art directors, and the art directors are winning. Everyone only wants to have a good time. They come here every year for the laughs and the fun. But looking at Tom James you'd think the survival of entire planet depended on his team's winning the game.

There he is standing on the mound getting ready to pitch with tears streaming down his face and screaming at the top of his lungs, "If you guys don't do better, you'll regret it." His eyes are bulging out of his head, his face twisted in pain.

He starts issuing orders, "Jones, get over there closer to third base. Schwartz, move in. Stevens, wake up, the play's at second."

I ask one of the art directors, "What's the score?"

"We're ahead by eight runs."

They are taunting Tom, "Tommy boy's a cry baby, Tommy boy's a cry baby." The more they tease him the more he cries, it's bizarrely frightening, like watching a grammar school game, with little 6-year olds.

They all know that in the office in the weeks to come, he will make it a point to get even with every member of the opposing team one by one. He's done it before.

What motivates this man? He is the most driven person I've ever met. What demons are constantly pushing him over the edge? I wonder what his background is? Plato once wrote quoting Socrates, *"Of madness there are two kinds; one produced by human infirmity, the other…a divine release of the soul from the yoke of custom and convention…The divine madness is subdivided into four kinds, prophetic, initiatory, poetic, and erotic, having four gods over them: the first was the inspiration of Apollo, the second that of Dionysus, the third that of the Muses, the fourth that of Aphrodite and Eros."*

Which one is Tom James? I think to myself.

Too scared to drink

Now, I'm just finishing a grueling morning-long photography session for the agency's large liquor account: "General Brands." They are the marketers of, among other things, the country's top selling vodka: "Saint Petersburg."

It's amazing how much time it can take to photograph a bottle of clear booze and a glass of it over ice. Every drip of moisture on the glass has to be absolutely perfect, every reflection and shadow sharp and crisp.

And the client, in this case Larry Ryan, is an absolute bastard. Nothing ever looks right to him, he's constantly complaining, "Can't you guys get it right, it's only a fucking bottle of crystal-clear vodka?"

You can tell a lot about a company's core culture by the way its employees treat their vendors. If people are not a bastard when they join the company they soon are coerced into becoming one.

Controlling the reflections and refractions, in glass, is a tedious job that can drive a person to drink.

The photographer, Tony Schwartz, is one of the best still-life photographers in the business. He is carefully cutting these tiny odd-shaped custom pieces of black and white paper, attaching them to light stands, placing them at various locations in space, surrounding the bottle to control the reflections the camera sees on the bottle. The scene resembles the pattern of black and white butterflies swirling to return to their nest. It takes hours and extreme patience. Thank goodness some smart prop guy came up with non-melting ice made from pieces of clear Lucite shaped like ice cubes. I can't imagine what they did before this fake ice; it must have been a nightmare having to replace the melting ice every few minutes under the hot lights. I'm glad I wasn't around at the time, especially with this client.

Thank goodness Al, the curmudgeonly, old copywriter on the account is here with me, to pacify Ryan.

As it turns out, the only reason the agency has this huge account is that Al is Larry's drinking buddy. And when I say: "drinking buddy," I mean everyday, breakfast, lunch, dinner, and beyond, drinking buddy.

I don't know how a person can have a drink at breakfast. Even the powerful, worldwide DDBO creative director Tom James hasn't been able to fire Al. Lord knows he's tried. Ryan keeps him around just for the fun of it.

"Al, I can't make lunch today, but I'll see you at the usual place at five, sharp, don't be late like the last time, you know I hate drinking alone. There's a lot of other agencies who are looking for my business," he verbally abuses Al, the company culture raising its ugly head again.

"I'll be there," Al responds, rolling his eyes to the ceiling, out of Larry's view.

The client heads out the door, but not before firing off one more salvo at us, "If this photo isn't right, you'll all have your asses in a sling."

"You'll like it, I guarantee," Al says, as he winks at me, again out of Larry's sight.

As soon as the client closes the door Al turns to me, "What say, we get some lunch at the Brass Rail, Bob?" He flashes his patented leprechaun grin.

"Where?"

"Right downstairs, come on I'll show you. Tony, you can finish up can't you? Send the photos over to Bob's office this afternoon."

"Sure thing, Al."

We exit the Clark building near the corner of 42nd Street and Fifth Avenue. Al takes a sharp right turn and directly into the Brass Rail Restaurant and bar. I never really noticed it was here, before.

I take a few steps through the right-hand door toward the host in the restaurant. As I walk along I hear a knocking on the glass partition to the left of me. It's Al, I didn't notice that he entered into the left-hand door into the bar. He motions for me to come into the bar and join him. I do so. Before I sit down on the stool next to him, the bartender sails a gigantic, double Martini glass to a perfect landing in front of Al.

"Thanks, Bill."

As I barely settle my butt into the soft cushion on the stool he guzzles it down and slides it back across the bar to the bartender, who has already made another and is carefully maneuvering it around the first to satisfy Al's Leprechaunian thirst.

"Order a drink, Randall."

"I don't want a drink, I want to eat."

"Tell him what you want, he'll get it for you."

"I'll have a hamburger, with onions and a glass of milk. What about you Al, what are you going to eat?"

"This is my lunch, hit me again, Bill."

Before my burger arrives, Al swallows his third martini and is out the door.

"I'll see you back at the office, Bob, take your time, put it on my tab, Bill."

"All right, Al, we'll see you later."

I am petrified of alcohol. My grandmother had put the fear of God in me. When she found out that I was going to work in the advertising business, she said: "Robert, you're going to become an alcoholic. The advertising business does it to everyone."

Her strong opinion came from television. She religiously watched a TV program called: "Sherman Billingly's Stork Club," that showed all the advertising people drinking themselves, sometimes, to death. It scared her, and she definitely scared me. I'm never going to drink.

After my grandparents died I had an epiphany. I came to realize that my drive, ambition and determination actually came from the early images put into my brain by my grandparents, aunts and uncles when I was a little boy. In addition to my grandmother's warning about alcohol, she would inspire me by pointing to the executives that Sherman Billingsly was interviewing on television and tell me that they make a lot of money and I could one day be one of them making over ten thousand dollars a year and have a big house. "They make a lot more money than your father and grandfather do as firemen, Robert," she used to say.

It impressed me so much that I kept that image of myself in my mind as I progressed into the field of advertising. I was actually pursuing more of my grandmother's goals for success than my own. Up to that point I hadn't really developed any goals of my own.

Later that day, I go to Al's office to drop off the layouts for the Saint Petersburg ads that contain the photos that we took this morning.

When I get to his office, the door is shut.

I push the door open and there is Al in his usual afternoon position snoring up a storm with his head down on his desk. I carefully place the layouts next to his head and exit the office pulling the door closed behind me. No one minds that Al spends every afternoon sleeping at his desk. He has to get some rest before the evening's drinking bout with Larry Ryan. Without him the agency would not have the General Brands account.

It's all a sick, crazy game

Now I'm suddenly entering the lobby on Fifth Avenue of the agency's largest client: Norman Cosmetics. I'm with Sandy Burnstein, the account supervisor and Roberta Ellison, the copywriter. I am now the youngest art director in the Norman Cosmetics group, Arty Stevens, my immediate boss, is on a photography assignment over in Rome, for Air Italy, one of the agency's other important accounts. I'm ordered to go with the copywriter and account executive to show layouts of the latest shade promotion ads to the owner of the company, Hal Norman. There is a standing order that no layout of any ad is to be shown to Mr. Norman unless there is an art director here to take down any changes and explain how they would be made or if they can't be, tell him why.

The lobby of the building is pure white marble with a giant, golden Norman Cosmetics logo floating on the wall surrounded by a display of Norman Cosmetics ads, each illuminated from behind.

We file into the first dazzling, all-white elevator I have ever seen. Even the carpet is white. It must be impossible to keep it clean on a rainy day. They probably have dozens of white carpets in the basement and rotate them from the elevators to the cleaners.

I am careful to follow Sandy's lead. I have a great deal of respect for Sandy; he is a bright man with great knowledge of the cosmetics business.

He leans over and whispers in my ear, "Bob-O, we're also presenting your mascara layouts today." He has pet names for all the people he works with at the agency.

I feel increased tension. I had no idea he was going to be presenting the layouts that I had finished yesterday for Norman's new waterproof mascara.

We exit on the 5th floor and enter the huge, almost sterile-looking reception room. Everything is white; the ceiling, the walls, the doors, the desk, the chairs, even the rug is white, like the elevator. It must be a lot tougher to keep clean because it can't be easily rotated.

Sandy sits down in one of the chairs next to the doors and takes off his shoes. So does Roberta.

"Bob-O, take off your shoes."

I do so and put them in a white box next to the chairs. We all stand silently, shoeless, in the pristine reception room.

"Mr. Burnstein, Mr. Norman will see you in two and a half minutes," the receptionist, who's clad, naturally, in a white dress and white slippers, announces.

We sit not saying a word. In exactly two and a half minutes, the receptionist rises, strolls over and opens the double-doors to Mr. Norman's office.

"Burnstein, I hope the new layouts are better than the last one's." The tall, overbearing man rising from behind an enormous, antique, white French provincial desk almost bellows in a crude tone sounding more like a longshoreman than a cosmetics company president.

Sandy ignores Mr. Norman's challenge, having heard them before, and courageously leads the way, tiptoeing into his office, sitting himself in the big white chair in front of Mr. Norman's desk. The door to the right of Mr. Norman's desk opens and in charges an oversized man who has the thick neck and broad shoulders of an old football player. "Sandy, why the hell didn't you tell me about this meeting?"

"I'm sorry Bill, I asked Mr. Norman's secretary to tell you."

"Well she didn't"

"Mr. Norman, this is Robert Randall, he's the new art director on your account."

"He looks like he's still wet behind the ears.

"He's a very talented art director."

The big bruiser flops into the chair next to Sandy.

"Robert, this is Bill Mendleson the director of marketing of Norman Cosmetics.

"Hello Bill, nice to meet you."

He doesn't acknowledge my presence, at all.

Sandy begins his presentation by taking the four, full-page size, four-color ads from the big black portfolio he has been carrying. I had comped the spread layouts to fit Vogue Magazine, the day before. They're based on Arty Stevens' brilliant graphic direction. I'm lucky to be working for him, all the other art directors in the agency are jealous, Arty is the new hot shot brought in to add his genius to the Norman Cosmetics account. These comprehensive layouts are variations for the latest shade promotion for the new "Arctic Ice" lipstick and nail polish. Each layout is mounted on, and surrounded by, a 4-inch border of gray matte board. Roberta motions for me to sit in one of the white tufted chairs next to her over by the wall.

Mr. Norman sits back down, leans forward resting his elbows on his desk and placing his hands under his chin, simultaneously wrinkling his brow down challengingly.

Sandy is not deterred; he begins to verbally present Arty Stevens' brilliant creative strategy behind the ads.

"Hal, the strategy behind these ads was developed by Roberta, here, and Arty Stevens.

"Where the hell is Arty Stevens?"

"He's on location."

"Where?"

"He's in Europe, getting some background photos for you to use in next year's "Around the World with Norman Cosmetics" campaign.

"Oh."

Now, these ads are designed as spreads for the fashion magazines and created to visually emphasize the name "Arctic Ice," in the consumer's mind. They are staged in an arctic setting, with rolling hills of North Pole snow stretching across the horizon in the background. There is an igloo in the foreground. The sky above is exploding with the brilliant colors of the Aurora Borealis. A beautiful model, clad in a white, furry parka is exiting from a white sleigh that is being pulled by six, white reindeer." Sandy reads the headline, "Beauty at the top of the world." Then he reads the tag line below the "Arctic Ice" tube of lipstick and nail enamel bottle, "A new, chillingly exciting shade from Norman Cosmetics."

Sandy continues to present each layout, carefully placing it on Mr. Norman desk.

Without saying a word, Mr. Norman takes each of the ads, which has the same elements, but in a different layout arrangement, looks at it for a few seconds and tosses it on the floor next to his desk. When Sandy finishes presenting all four layouts, Mr. Norman stands up abruptly, stretches his arms over his head, yawning and pronouncing his disdain for the whole process.

"What dreck."

"Dreck," echoes his underling Bill Mendleson.

He then begins stomping on, and kicking, the layouts he doesn't like across the room, one at a time.

"This is shit," he says as he boots the first one.

"I hate this one, she's ugly," he says referring to the choice of model used in the second ad.

"You didn't use my "Century Schoolboy" on this one," he shouts, referring to the fact that I had not used "Century Schoolbook," the typeface he prefers on all his ads.

It's a totally frightening experience for me. I have never been subjected to this kind of direct rudeness from another human being in my life before, let alone from the agency's most important client. I know it is critical that I not react to his outburst. I just sit in my chair trying to look intelligent, neither smiling nor looking unhappy.

"Robert, do you have any suggestions?" Sandy asks me, looking totally unruffled by Mr. Norman's obnoxious performance.

I muster up some courage and slowly walk over to the pile of disheveled layouts and pick them up one at a time.

"I can change the model on this one, Mr. Norman."

"And I will change the type to Century Schoolbook." I sheepishly offer.

"What's your name, Randall is it? Do it quick, and get them back here this afternoon, if you want to keep your job. Throw the other two into the garbage."

"I have brought head sheets of several other models for you to look at, just in case."

"This is a smart kid you got here, Sandy."

I take the head sheets out of the envelope I am carrying and hand them to Mr. Norman.

He flips through the six 8 by 10 photos, picks one and throws the rest in the fancy white waste basket next to his desk.

"This is the one, does she have big tits?"

I feel embarrassed for Roberta. I look at her and she motions her head for me to answer Mr. Norman.

"Look on the back or the head sheet Mr. Norman, her measurements are there."

"36, 24, 35", he reads out loud, "okay, use her;" he spins the photo across the room to me.

"Forget the parka, I want her in a sexy dress with her tits bulging out of the top."

"Which photographer are you going to use?"

"Richard Avalon."

"I've heard of him. How much are you guys going to pay him?"

"He gets a thousand dollars a day plus expenses."

"Pay him 3 thousand."

"3 thousand?"

"That's right, I want him to be paid more than any other photographer in the world when he works for Norman Cosmetics. So anytime you call him and tell him you want him to do a photo for Hal Norman at Norman Cosmetics, he'll jump at it."

"Yes, sir."

"Now, get out, all of you."

"We'll have the revised layout back here this afternoon," Sandy confirms.

"You bet your ass you will,"

"Do you have time to go over the layout and copy for the mascara ad?"

"Bring it back this afternoon, Burnstein."

"Mr. Norman, the price of the mascara has gone up 10-cents a gross," Bill says.

"Sandy, raise the price in the ad 10-cents each." Mr. Norman orders.

I make a note to change the price on the ad for this afternoon's meeting. I feel relieved, I'm glad I don't have to experience his maniacal reaction to my mascara layout. Sandy will present it without me.

On the way back to the office in the cab, Sandy tries to give me some background to explain Mr. Norman's abusive performance, "Bob-O, he came from a poor, rural family. He and his brother started out selling nail polish door-to-door. They experienced great rejection. It caused him to become a hard-driving perfectionist whose imperious personality leads most of his business associates to sever their connections with him very quickly."

"Why do we have to put up with it?"

"Because that's what we get paid for."

"Robert, this is all good experience for you, learn from it." Roberta adds.

The horny dentist

Vic Ennis' face suddenly appears in my brain. He's an old-time art director who has been in the agency for over 20-years and who has turned down being promoted any higher because he knows he can't handle responsibility. He comes running into the bullpen we share in the "Connelly's Soup" group.

"The dentist is in!"

"What dentist?" I ask, completely puzzled.

"The one across the street. Come on, I'll show you what I'm talking about."

He leads the way to the corner office of the head art director, Steve Svenson, who is on vacation at the moment. The office is crowded with over a dozen account executives, art directors and copywriters, all leering out the window, focusing on a single window in the building across Madison Avenue.

As we enter Vic shouts his famous corny line: "What are your nuts hanging out the window?" The guys give their usual exaggerated laugh-reaction.

"What's going on?" I ask.

"Yellow brick building 8th floor 3rd window from the left," Roger Dowd, one of the copywriters announces, pointing his finger across the street.

I scan to find what they all are looking at.

"8th floor 3rd window from the left," Roger repeats.

Then I see it. The dentist is doing his nurse in his dentist's chair. He doesn't appear to have a clue that anyone is watching him.

"I can't believe he doesn't know we're over here looking at him." I naively comment.

"He does it every day at this exact same time," Roger says in a know-it-all tone. "She must pencil herself in on his appointment calendar."

"Wow, will you look at that, he's actually mounting her on his dentist chair?" Nick DiNapoli exclaims in a loud voice that the secretaries in the first cubicle outside most likely can hear.

Nick is one of the old time account executives, a flashy, loveable guy who likes to spend money, especially when it's not his. His boss, Paul McNamara, a tall thin guy with extreme pride in his Irish heritage, goes over Nick's expense account every month with a fine toothcomb. Paul makes him sit and account for every item and every receipt. Nick's a medium sized guy who has to shave his head every morning because he is almost totally bald. The girls love him and frequently kiss him on his shinny "chrome dome" to leave their lipstick brands. Nick swings through Brooks Bothers every day on his way to lunch, just to make sure he's up to snuff on his wardrobe. The 21 Club is his regular hangout. He has his own, private table there. The clients all love him. And he is a fanatic when it comes to his body. He exercises five times a week. The girls like that too.

"This is great." The newest account executive, Gary Miller, yells as he elbows his way to the front of the pack. Gary's from Missouri, where he grew up on a farm, a farm that actually has its own cemetery. He talks about how he spent most of his youth "plinking" at rabbits with his .22-rifle and castrating cows. He's a little sensitive about his middle name, "Lee." A basic "meat and potatoes" kind of guy, he is still totally awed by the big city. When he walks down the street he's constantly staring up at the skyscrapers squeezing his pointed chin with his hand in total awe. Where he comes from, there is nothing but flat farmland stretching to the horizon in every direction. Everybody likes him; he has a square, chiseled jaw, dark brown hair and brooding "cow" eyes. He looks a lot like Cary Grant, and the girls are all after him because they think he'd make the perfect husband. His father gave him the choice of taking over the family farm or going to college. He chose college. "This is great, who's got a pair of binoculars?"

"Hey Gary, give somebody else a chance, Vic yells.

One summer day, when we were cruising down 5th Avenue at lunchtime checking out the new wave of bra-less chicks that the new women's movement was inspiring, Gary told me about the time he brought his special girlfriend, Carole, to the farm. His mother asked her if she liked chicken. She said yes. His mother disappeared for a few minutes. She returned to the kitchen from the chicken house with two plump chickens, one fluttering in each hand.

"How do these look, Carole?"

"Oh my, they're huge."

His mother then proceeded to simultaneously swing them up into the air over her head bringing them down with great force, snapping their necks. They continued to flap their wings, even after she adroitly cut off their heads.

"Oh, my," is all that Carole could say. "Oh, my."

Suddenly Ralph Hill, the head of the print production department, comes charging in. "What's up boys?"

He knows very well what's up; he has an uncanny sense when it comes to anything to do with sex. He pushes his way to the front of the crowd, pulling his huge binoculars from his jacket pocket.

"8th floor 3rd window from the left," Roger announces again.

"Let me have a look," Ralph says as he focuses his binoculars.

"Wow, she looks like a contortionist, look at that position."

"Let me have a look, Ralph?" Roger asks.

"Are you kidding, these are mine, get your own."

"Vic, I think I've wasted enough time, I've got work to do," I say.

"I'm going over to that building to see if I can find that dentist's office and get a closer look at that nurse," Ralph declares.

"Now, don't queer the deal for everybody. If the dentist finds out we know about his "afternooners," it'll be over, and they'll be a lot of unhappy campers over here," Roger warns him.

"I got to get back to work. I've got an ad that I have to take over to the client this afternoon," Gary announces, pushing his way back out through the crowd of leering lechers. "Thanks for the invite, guys."

I follow him out of the office and we head back to our cubicles.

"Bet you don't get much of this kind of action back in Missouri."

"No, back there it's just the stallions mounting the mares."

Gary has a very dry sense of humor.

Watering holes

The whole bar scene appears in my head. At the end of the day there are really two bar scenes – one is mostly the tired, worn out old guys on their way home to their families in the bedroom towns north of New York City like Scarsdale, Westport, and New Canaan – the other crowd is a combination of the younger guys looking to get laid along with the secretaries looking for husbands. Most of the younger group lives in the City so they pick the classier bars on Madison Avenue.

The older crowd begins their afternoon ritual by sneaking out of their offices as early as 4:00 p.m. and heading to Grand Central Station, each to their own favorite watering hole. There are dozens and dozens of them surrounding Grand Central. The waiters in these places get to know their customers so well that starting around 6 p.m. they begin calling out the times, destinations and track numbers of their regulars' trains; "George, the 6:12 to Westport is boarding on track 10." Most just nod and order another drink. "I'll catch the next one, Harry," is the standard response.

Meanwhile the young studs and the husband hunters take up positions in their favorite watering holes. The tone is much more boisterous, upbeat and fun. They are at the beginning of their lives and looking toward the future with great excitement and enthusiasm. The advertising business hasn't yet worn them out and forced them to their knees. Their bars are filled with jokes, laughter and dreams of sex and romance. I abhor both groups, especially the older guys, beaten men trying to avoid going home at all cost. Their lives squeezed between jobs they hate and wives they hate, drinking until the last train is called. As he stumbles to the door, Lou Newman shouts, "I don't want to get home until after those God-damned kids are in bed."

Harry Conroy, one of the waiters at The Grand Central Bar, rushes up to a table of DDBOers and announces, "Charlie, it's Tom James on the phone, he sounds really pissed-off, he wants you back in the office right away."

That's another one of the things that ingratiates Tom James to all of his subordinates; he has the phone number of every bar around Grand Central Station where DDBO employees hang out. He even knows the names of the waiters. Tom is such a conniving person he had his secretary Mildred compile a complete list of bars, waiters and even possible DDBO personnel who patronize each place.

"Tell him I'm not here, Harry."

"I already told him you were."

"Brilliant, what the hell did you do that for? There goes your tip."

"He threatened to come over here and get you in person, and if he shows up I'd lose all my DDBO customers."

"Tell him I'll see him in the morning."

"He said to tell you that if you don't come back to the office tonight, don't bother coming to work in the morning."

"Someday somebody's going to murder that fucking son-of-a-bitch."

I am one of the lucky ones I had already found my future-wife so my life is focused entirely on getting ahead. Almost every day the creative guys would surround my drawing board and try to convince me to go down to the bars with them. I think they were motivated by two reasons; first they didn't like my showing them up by working harder than them, and they also wanted my money to pay the tab. They knew I worked every night to get money for a down payment for a house. I had a clear, positive vision of my future married life. Many of the guys tried to poison my mind about marriage. "The first thing you have to do, Robert, is take control of the checkbook. The man should be in control of the money." Ned Johnson one of the other art directors proclaimed.

"My wife is working, she has as much right to our money as I do."

"Are you out of your mind, women are trying to take over the world, we can't let them do that."

"Why are you guys so insecure?"

"Come on, Robert, come down for a drink with us."

"I've got work to do, for a meeting first thing in the morning. See you guys tomorrow."

Kiss your career goodbye

I see Tom James come running into my cubicle. I'm the assistant art director to Paul Kennedy, considered by most of the agency to be the best art director at DDBO.

"Here, Randall, I want these layouts redone. They're shit," Tom shouts, as he tosses a pile of Paul's layouts onto my drawing board.

"Tom, I didn't do these."

"I know, your loser of a boss did them. They're shit I can't show them to the client, we'll lose the account."

"Tell Paul. If he says it's okay, I'll do them over."

"Bull shit, you do them or I'll have your job."

I get up from my drawing table and march straight into Paul Kennedy's office.

"Where do you think you're going Randall?"

"Paul, Tom James needs these layouts redone right away and I can do them."

"Where is he?"

"He's in my cubicle and he's steaming."

Paul gets up and stomps across the hall.

"What the hell is going on here, Tom?"

"Your layouts are shit, I'm not going to bring them to the client"

"I've been working on this account for 20-years and my layouts have made a lot of money for this agency."

"These layouts look like they were done 20-years ago."

"What changes do you want to make, let's sit down and discuss them."

"I don't have time for that, just let Randall redo them so I can get out of here. He knows what the client wants."

"Paul, I have some time I can do them."

"Okay Robert, thanks."

"Tom, I'm going to speak to Sven about this."

"Don't threaten me you fucking dinosaur, I'll have your job."

"I'm still the art director on this account."

"It's time to get out of the way, us Young Turks are taking over."

"We'll see about that."

Paul stomps back into his office and slams his door.

"All right, Randall, I'll be back in 30-minutes to get the layouts."

"I'll do the best I can, Tom."

"Randall, you better start thinking about whose side you're on. You're either with me or against me, make up your mind."

Tom James rushes out of my cubicle and down the hall toward his office. I have never met a more confrontational person.

The door to Paul Kennedy's office opens, "Robert, can I see you for a second?"

I jump up and cross to his office.

"That son of a bitch, Tom James pushed me too far that time."

"Don't worry about it, I'll get the layouts done."

"Thanks, Robert, I really appreciate it."

He takes a long drag on his cigarette, tilts his head all the way back runs his hand through his long, wavy gray hair and blows the smoke up toward the ceiling in a slow, deliberate exhale.

"Someday, I'm going to kill that bastard."

"Paul, you may want to back off a bit, he has been building his political strength at DDBO and getting anyone in his way fired."

"Randall, you're too much of a softy, you're not going to get anywhere in this business."

I just look at him and wonder what the future holds for the both of us.

This conflict reminds me of the complexity of life and Plato's "The Inner Man." *"Beauty depends on simplicity – I mean the true simplicity of a rightly and nobly ordered mind and character. He is a fool who seriously inclines to weigh the beautiful by any other standard than that of the good. The good is beautiful. Grant me to be beautiful in the inner man."*

Where will I be in the struggle to see the beauty of life?

D.O.A.

I'm now reliving the sad story of Bill Harris, the Account Supervisor on the Norman Cosmetics account before Sandy Burnstein.

It's two-thirty in the morning in the fashionable bedroom town of Westport, Connecticut.

Westport has become the favorite hometown of most of the top executives in the New York advertising community because they're the only ones who can afford the fancy homes on the large plots of land.

Bill Harris is tossing and turning in his bed as he does every night of his life. He took the Account Supervisor job on the notoriously difficult Norman Cosmetics account to pay the tuition for his kid's educations, the payments on his two new cars, the country club dues, the Nantucket vacations and the monster mortgage he had to take out to get this house in Westport. There's no question he knows he's way overextended and he spends most of his days, and all of his nights lying awake, worrying about losing his job.

The phone rings, Bill jumps to his feet and grabs the phone, "Hello, this is Bill Harris."

"Who the hell is that, at this hour?" His wife Anne snarls, knowing full well who it is.

"Yes, Mr. Norman, what can I do for you?"

Bill pauses and sits down on the edge of the bed.

"Now?" Bill asks with his hand cupping the mouthpiece as he whispers into the phone, hoping his wife doesn't hear him.

"Tell him you'll see him in the morning, Bill."

"Let me take this on the other phone in my study, Mr. Norman."

As Bill disappears from the bedroom, his wife sits up and calls to him, "Bill, where the hell are you going at this hour?"

"It's okay, Honey, go back to sleep. You can hang up the phone now," he says as he enters his study and closes the door behind him.

Before his wife hangs up the phone, she hears Mr. Norman yelling at Bill; "Harris, you get your ass down here to El Morocco immediately! I want to discuss our new advertising budget. If your not interested, I'm sure I can find another agency that is," growls Norman.

Anne is tempted to tell Mr. Norman off but she knows it would mean Bill's job. Bill comes back into the bedroom and hastily begins getting dressed.

"You're not going out at this hour." Bills wife threatens, knowing full well what his answer will be.

"Mr. Norman wants to discuss the new budget, I've got to go."

"At this hour, is he crazy?" his wife barks, "I'm not going to let you go."

"I've got to go, or he'll fire us," Bill laments, as he finishes dressing.

"There aren't any trains at this hour," his wife yells, as she gets angrier and angrier.

"Shhhh, you'll wake up the kids. I'll have to drive. It shouldn't take long at this time of night. Besides, you know I can't afford to lose my job right now we're so far in debt." Bill almost pleads with his wife to let him go. "We'd lose everything, honey."

"Don't you see what this is doing to your health?"

"I have no choice," Bill whimpers, tears coming to his eyes, "I have to go."

"Well, it's your funeral." Bill's wife yells as he tiptoes down the stairs to the garage.

Within an hour he pulls up in front of El Morocco.

"Unusual to see you at this hour, Mr. Harris," the doorman says.

"Is Mr. Norman still inside, Paul?"

"Yes, sir, at his usual table, and he's in a really foul mood, too."

"I know," Bill gets out of the car, handing a ten-dollar bill to the doorman, "That's the reason I'm here."

"Thanks, Mr. Harris," The doorman hands Bill a little blue ticket for his car.

"Good evening, Mr. Harris," the hat check girl says as he almost runs by her to get to Mr. Norman's table. The show music is blaring in the background.

Mr. Norman is at his regular table next to the huge palm trees and colorful sashes that are supposed to simulate the inside of a Sheiks tent in the desert of Morocco. There's a blond seated on each side of him.

"It's about time you got here Harris, you've kept me waiting over an hour," Mr. Norman shouts over the exotic music.

"Sorry, Mr. Norman, I got here as quickly as I could."

"Well, you took so long to get here, I don't have time to talk with you now, meet me at my office at eight in the morning, let's go girls," Mr. Norman says, as he gets up and abruptly leaves the restaurant with a girl on each arm.

Bill doesn't have the strength to respond. He just spins around, grabs his chest, slumps over the fancy red, padded chair at the table, and dies from a massive heart attack. The loud Moroccan desert music never stops.

His wife was right it was his own funeral he was going to.

Bill's life insurance policies will put his kids through school; pay off the car loans, and the mortgage too.

Anne will probably have to give up the country club membership and the vacations in Nantucket and go back to work.

His family is all set, and maybe Bill is too.

I'm starting to see what a nasty business advertising can be.

Martin Mayer in *"Madison Avenue, U.S.A."* wrote: *"Advertising men rarely get much time away from their jobs. They work in a windy atmosphere of shifting preferences, where crisis is a normal state of affairs and as one advertising manager put it, 'somebody is always hitting the panic button.' Every night the brief cases and attaché cases go home stuffed with work, because the advertising man is paid for his production, not his time and the industry expects every man to do his duty whether he is in the office or eating lunch, on the commuter train or in the bosom of his family. A man who worked for J. Sterling Getchell, the blazing meteor of the advertising business said: '…you didn't dare have a telephone at home. You'd get home from the office at 1:00 a.m. and just as you were dropping off to sleep the phone would ring, it would be Getch, he wanted to check something with you."*

A life preserver for a drowning drinker

My mind jumps to one afternoon at DDBO, Sandy Burnstein comes running into my cubicle, "Bob-O, we need a tune-in ad and we need it fast."

It is my job to design all the tune-in ads for the Norman Cosmetics weekly quiz show: "The Big Money Question." Each week there is a new ad based on the results of last week's program, and featuring this week's surviving contestant.

"Bob-O, I can't find Roselyn anywhere. She was supposed to have the copy for this ad two days ago, and I've got to get the layout over to Hal Norman in two hours."

"Alright Sandy, let me see what I can do." I try to calm him down.

"Do you think you can help me?"

"Give me about 20-minutes and I'll come up with an ad for you."

"You think you can you do it, Bob-O, the copy too?" He says with a tone of desperation in his voice.

"Yes, I'm sure I can, come back in 20-minutes."

"Okay, I'm going to call the client and tell him I'll be over with the ad by 2 p.m.," he says, with a big sigh of relief.

I get right to work. It's a good thing I watch the show every week,

I know exactly what has happened. I pull out a layout bond pad and draw out the size of the newspaper ad in the center of the page. It's a 900-line ad; 3-columns wide by 300-lines deep.

I stop, grab the phone and call Sandy's secretary; I want to confirm the name of the last winner, "Lori, what is the name of the big winner from last weeks show?"

"Larry Perkins, he's a shoemaker from Brooklyn, New York. He won $10,000."

"Got it, thanks, bye."

I start by lettering in the headline I have written, in black charcoal pencil.

"Tune in Tonight at 8 p.m., on WABC-TV. Watch Larry Perkins, a shoemaker from Brooklyn, New York, as he attempts to climb his way from $10,000 to the Jackpot prize of $50,000. Will he make it? Find out Tonight!"

Next I sketch in a likeness of Larry Perkins standing beside the show's host, Mike Harold, on the stage next to the famous soundproof booth. I rough in lines of copy, add the Norman Cosmetics and WABC-TV logos and I'm done with the layout.

I quickly write 30-words of descriptive copy and race to the secretary's section at the entrance to the art department.

"Claire can I use your typewriter?"

"What is it you need typed, Robert?"

"I have to type out this copy I have written for this Norman Cosmetics tune-in ad."

"Copy you wrote? I'll do it for you, it'll only take me a minute."

Claire is the daughter of a wealthy New York family who is also in the cosmetics business. She sits down and starts clicking away.

"This is excellent copy, Robert, did you really write it?"

"Yes I did. Sandy Burnstein needs the ad right away, and Roselyn's down in her usual corner booth at 'Cherry's.'"

In less than a minute and a half, Claire declares: "I'm done."

"Thanks, Claire, I really appreciate it."

"Any time, Robert." She hands me the copy and

I decide to take the ad down to Sandy's office instead of calling him to come up for it. I hop into the elevator, and go down to the fifth floor. As the doors open I'm about to bolt to Sandy's office, when I hear his voice coming from the other end of the reception room.

"Bob-O, I'm over here, let's see it."

I push the layout and copy into his hands,

"Wow, great job, Bob-O, they're going to love it. You are my hero, see you later."

He puts his brief case on the receptionist's desk, snaps the locks, pops it open, puts the copy and layout inside and bolts to the elevator.

Over the next months I did all the writing and designing of all the Norman Cosmetics tune-in ads.

I loved it and it helped Roselyn Cronin, the regular copywriter of the tune-in ads. She had turned to alcohol after her son was killed in an auto accident last year. She comes to work every morning, goes down to the restaurant-bar on the street level of the building at 10 a.m., and spends the rest of the day mourning her son. I feel sorry for her and do all I can to help her get through her problem. Tom James has made it known, that if he catches her unable to work again he's going to fire her, on the spot. I don't want her to get fired; it would probably kill her. Maybe that's what she wants.

Larry Watson tells me he loves me

My mind flashes to the hallway outside of Larry Watson's office. I'm a new young art director and he's an experienced senior art director. He is the Art Group Head of the Hydra Fibers account. He's a tall, quiet, extremely introverted, overly thin man of about 40. He has a soft voice with a distinguished southern accent, gained from the growing up in an upscale community in the southern part of Virginia.

I'm about to go do my first shoot with the world's most famous photographer, Richard Avelon and I'm scared shitless. Oh, I've done photo sessions with many other photographers, but not with the most famous one in the whole world.

Larry's face appears over the frosted-glass top to my cubicle wall, "Bob, will you please come into my office for a minute?"

I assume he wants to prepare me for the shoot with Richard Avelon.

I follow Larry into his office. "Larry, I'm a little nervous about this shoot, a lot is riding on these pictures, and I'm not as sure of myself as I would like everyone to believe I am, going onto this expensive location shooting."

"Don't you worry, your going to do just fine, Bob. I know you can do it. I have the utmost confidence in you. You are an extremely talented art director. Please shut the door."

"But what is it like to work with Richard Avelon?"

"He's the same as any other photographer. A professional who wants you to look good, so he looks good."

"I have told him that you are a new art director with outstanding talent and sensitivity. He's anxious to work with you."

"Thank you, I appreciate your talking to him about me."

"I also told him I love you."

"What?"

"That's right Bob, I love you."

I'm flabbergasted I don't know what to say I sit speechless.

"Bob, I have loved you from the day you came into my group."

I'm still silent, and getting a little scared. I'm trying to understand exactly what he is saying. I know he is married with a daughter. I just don't know how to handle this situation.

"Larry, I don't know what to say, I respect you and I like you a lot, I just don't know what to say."

"Bob, I'm sorry to hit you with this. I had a rough upbringing. My father was a doctor and he never gave me much time. He never showed me any love and he and my mom divorced when I was 12. When I graduated from high school, I hated him so much that I didn't want to ever see him again, so I demanded that he give me my inheritance. He was reluctant at first, but finally gave in and I got $70,000. That was a lot of money back in 1938. I blew it all, every penny, on stupid things like fast cars, motorcycles, and drugs. I was a very angry young man, trying to find love in inanimate objects, and always getting into fights at the biker bars. I once almost died from a beating. My life wasn't working out. Then I met Charlotte; she changed my whole life, she straightened me out. When our daughter was born I was forced to grow up. Thank God, or I'd be dead."

I'm feeling panicked inside. How do I fit into this? What should I do, what should I say?

"Larry, I've got to be going, I have a meeting with Richard Avelon about the shoot."

"Okay, Bob, we'll talk later."

We never talked about it again.

Larry later transferred to the Chicago office and I never saw him again.

But I never forgot that day in his office.

Secrets of madness

I'm in a Hydra Fibers group meeting in Tom James' office. Suddenly Tom begins to cry like a baby, just as he did on the baseball diamond at the company outing. Again, he looks like a little boy. He abruptly jumps up and runs out of the office. We all sit with puzzled looks on our faces. As he leaves I look back and see a puddle on his chair that is beading and running off letting droplets fall on the floor. Tom had peed in his pants. I remember in 2nd grade, there was a boy, Donald Kenneth, who peed in his pants at least once a week. The teacher said not to make fun of him he couldn't help it. He would outgrow it. I guess Tom never did.

The advertising business like all businesses is mired in a secret madness that everyone knows about but no one ever talks about. They are desperately struggling to get the public to believe that advertising is an honest, straightforward industry with happy workers pursuing the "American dream." Nothing is further from the truth. It is discouraging and depressing to realize that nothing is what it seems to be, that hidden behind every action and decision, sick, mentally unbalanced business politics is pulling the strings. Kickbacks, payola, bribes, hookers, threats and even murder, are all merely tools of the trade. The advertising industry, more than any other is a master of deceit. The whole business was founded on an organized system of kickbacks; the agencies would receive payment for their work in the form of commissions from the magazines, newspapers, radio stations and television stations, rather than payments from the clients. It's a business that ravenously devours normal, kind, pleasant people like so much intestinal fodder and then evacuates them to a vast pile of human waste. Stress, ulcers, alcoholism, suicide, paranoia, fear, and mental illness are all hidden realities. It's amazing that anyone ever gets anything done in such a dark, slimy underworld of madness. Perhaps there are a few who are immune to all the insanity and just chug along doing their jobs.

The firing squads

Suddenly I'm thinking about the agency firing squads.

Getting fired, getting the pink slip, getting the boot, tying on the can, there are many ways to refer to a company getting rid of an employee. In the advertising business there are some companies that have sick, weird, almost draconian techniques to let someone know there employment services are no longer needed, especially when it comes to letting the higher-level executives go.

It's clear there are "squads" of people conjuring up these mentally disturbing approaches.

One company's so-called secret policy was to place the employee's clothes-tree in the hall outside their office door, so the unsuspecting worker would be signaled, long before he got to his office, that he was about to be let go. Of course, this approach was subjected to many practical jokes, before it was replaced by and even stranger and more bizarre technique.

In the case of one agency, the firing communications style was insidiously subtle but very devastating. An executive vice-president at one of the city's biggest agencies was in the habit of getting in to work early. On the momentous morning he followed his usual routine; a short stroll from Grand Central Station, a stop at his favorite tobacco stand in the lobby to get a fresh pack of cigarettes, an uneventful ride up in the elevator and into the reception room. "Good morning, Mr. Rosser."

"Good morning, Judy."

After a brisk walk to his office, he stops and turns the key in the lock. The door swings open and he steps in. But this morning, something is radically wrong. He senses it immediately, that his foot takes an extra fraction of a second to hit the top of his plush carpet. He knows instantly he is done for. The pad has been removed from under the carpet in his office during the night, a clear indication that it's all over for him. In some cases, this company has an even more sinister early warning system. They will go into the targeted employee's office in the middle of the night and remove two of his four side chairs. If the victim doesn't get the message, they move to the rug pad removal stage. Here again, practical jokes abound.

In one extreme case, a top executive had been on vacation. When he returned, he noticed he wasn't greeted with the usual warm, "welcome back" from vacation. Fellow employees just smiled or grinned nervously. He began his long trek down the corridor to his office on the window side of the building. Suddenly, he was at the corner of the hallway. He spins around and looks back. He must have missed it. Now even more deliberately he marches back toward the reception room looking for his black nametag on the wall next to his office door. Nothing.

His office was gone. He knew that it meant he was a goner. He trudged down to the personnel department to get the official word. His boss didn't have the guts to tell him. They just sealed off the entrance to his office as if it had never been there.

The end of the line for two-hundred

I quickly flash to the day that became known as "Black Friday" at DDBO. It's a horrible scene; no one even had an inkling that it was going to happen. Apparently it was all the result of the Boston office getting the $10 million Meriweather Computer account by promising to buy one of their largest computers. The computer they get is so large that it fills a room over 50- by 50-feet in size. Management apparently didn't fully comprehend at the time, that the computer would make over four hundred bookkeepers obsolete the day it was up and running. When the agency woke up to what was actually about to happen, they began secretly installing the computer down on the second floor. They put it in an out-of-the-way space they had sublet from the publisher of American Home magazine, one of the agency's clients and a tenant in the building. When today came they never said a word, they merely put the pink slips in each bookkeeper's pay envelope, ordering them to leave the premises immediately. Word spread throughout the agency in minutes. Everyone in the agency is panicked and afraid to open his or her own pay envelopes. It's the kind of blood bath that is obviously going to be repeated, hundreds and hundreds of times over, during the next several years, throughout the industry, as agencies make the move to computers. It is the brutal price of entering the new age of computer technology. I'll never forget "Black Friday" at DDBO, the day 85-percent of the bookkeeping department got their pink slips.

The holiday lechers

Now I'm back to my first December 24, at DDBO, I step off the elevator into a mob of DDBOers doing a "Christmas conga line" through the lobby. They're singing "Jingle Bells," wearing Santa Claus hats and waving plastic glasses full of booze, all in tempo to the lyric. It's 8:30 in the morning and they're drinking already. This is my first time experiencing the-day-before-Christmas celebration at DDBO. As I head to my cubicle to hang up my coat one of the female revelers grabs my arm and tries to get me into the line with her. She thrusts a glass of hard liquor into my face. I pull away and continue to my drawing board. As I round the corner past Sven Svenson's office, he calls out to me, "Merry Christmas, Robert, have a drink." He's standing behind his desk with a glass in his hand. Spread out before him are at least a dozen different bottles of hard liquor, all the client's brands. This apparently is a DDBO Christmas tradition. Every Department Head has booze in their office for their people.

"No thanks, Mr. Svenson, I've got some layouts to do."

"Forget them it's Christmas, and call me Sven."

What a contrast to the images in my mind of Dickens' "Christmas Carol," here bosses and workers are hugging, singing and laughing together, having a good time.

"I'll have a ginger ale, please."

"Ginger ale?" remarks Claire, the art department secretary, as she comes over and plants a big kiss on my lips, definitely shaking me up a lot. "Merry Christmas, Robert."

"Thanks," I take the ginger ale and go to my drawing board to work on the layouts as a swarm of hecklers dance into my cubicle, surround me and begin singing "Jingle Bells," even louder.

"Come on, Bob, we've got to make the rounds, this it the only time of year you get to meet all the top brass of the agency. Let's go," Dom Martinetti implores.

I have no choice but to follow them. They dance and sing their way down to the executive floor and over to the other side of the building to where the president's office suite is located, and Dom and I follow. As we approach the doorway to the president's office, we can see it's jam-packed with DDBOers, all fighting to get in. The fact that most of them have all ready had too much to drink accelerates the pandemonium to a higher level.

Apparently this is the time of year when all the office lechers, both men and women, get to have a good time with each other. Living out their sexual fantasies from the past year.

I decide not to fight the crowd, but to get away from them, so I leave Dom and the reveling crowd and walk down to the other corner office on the executive floor where it's a little quieter. The corner offices are where the big shots are housed, of course. I'm not sure whose office is in this far corner, there doesn't seem to be anyone around this end of the building. The door to the office is closed. There is a nameplate next to the door with the name Donald Charles on it. He's the executive vice president of the agency and on the board of directors, an account guy who heads up the consumer products group. I've been in a couple of meetings with him. My curiosity gets the better of me; I think I'll take a look in his office. I slowly open the door and much to my chagrin there on the couch is Donald Charles, with his back to me, on top of a young woman who must be his secretary. She is yelling out in ecstasy, "Oh, yes, oh, yes, oh, yes." I begin to withdraw from the office when she leans her head to the side and sees me. She just gives me a big smile and a wink while she continues to let the executive vice president ride, screaming even louder. I can smell her perfume all the way over here at the door. It's L'amaint by Coty. I know it well; I've worked on the account.

Then my mind jumps to many years later when I run into Donald Charles in a bookstore at the airport. He greets me graciously, "Bob, it's so good to see you. Thank you so much for helping my son Bill find a job in Boston, I really appreciate it."

"Your more than welcome, Donald, he's a good young man."

He grins and looks over my shoulder at someone behind me.

"Oh Bob, have you met my wife, Millie?"

I turn around and there standing at a bookrack smiling at me in the same way she did in his office back when I was a fledgling art director at DDBO and she was servicing her boss, is his secretary.

"Millie, it's so good to meet you," is the only lame thing I can think of to say.

She walks over to me and gives me a kiss on the cheek. I know my face turned red.

"It's good to see you, again, Robert," she reaches out and squeezes my hand tightly.

Donald moves closer to me to whisper in my ear, I'm about to have a heart attack, I think he's going to mention my intrusion into his private life all those years ago. "Robert, I heard about the trouble you had with Tom James in the Regal Hotels meeting. I'm sorry about that, Tom was a very troubled person at that time in his life. You did the right thing."

"Thank you, Donald, I appreciate your sharing that with me."

"Well Millie, we've got to catch a plane, good to see you Bob."

"Yes, it's so nice to meet you, Bob," Millie surreptitiously gives me a wink, and she and Donald stroll back out of my life.

"Himself" Number One

Now I'm envisioning the sartorially splendid image of the obnoxious Richard Zimmerman, the infamous real estate mogul. His octopus of a company owns a lot of Manhattan Island, from brownstones to skyscrapers. He could put his company anywhere in the city, but chose to locate his personal office on the top floor of this building because it enabled him to build the only office in the city that rotates on a turntable with the sun, so the sun is always shining into his office all day long.

DDBO is the largest tenant occupying most of 385 Madison Avenue, however, this one person is convinced he is more important than even the chief executive officer of DDBO.

To announce his level of importance to the world, as if his P.T. Barnum costume alone isn't enough, every morning when he arrives in the lobby of the building, the elevator starter instantly empties whatever elevator is open to the consternation and grumbling of its bleary-eyed passengers. Even the president of DDBO has been asked to exit the elevator. One morning Tom James, the "Himself," of DDBO, refused to budge from the elevator, and the other "Himself," Richard Zimmerman, had to have another elevator emptied to satisfy his ego. There were two elevators worth of weeping and gnashing of teeth left cooling in the lobby that morning.

Looking very much like the famous circus owner, Mr. Zimmerman is decked out in a sparklingly shinny, black top hat, formal tuxedo, white shirt, bow tie, gray vest, long "Morning Coat," and striped gray pants leading down to gleaming black paten leather shoes snuggly covered by a pair of bright-white button-down spats. His appearance is replete with a pearl-topped cane that he twirls "Charlie Chaplin" style as he saunters across the lobby to the freshly emptied elevator.

"Thank you, my good man," he says, as he strolls into the center of the elevator passing out a crisp fifty-dollar bill to both the starter and operator.

Not too many years later, after his real estate empire collapsed in total ruins, he not only didn't have a revolving office, he didn't have his funny costume or any fifty-dollar bills to flaunt. He wasn't even allowed into the building. Life is funny sometimes, sometimes it's sad, and sometimes it's both at the same time.

Fast talker

"I love that painting, Bob."

Now I hear the fastest talker in the agency, Bradley Glenn, declare his love for my painting as he storms abruptly into my office.

"Oh?"

"What do you call it?"

"Montauk Point."

"I've always loved that painting. I stop in to look at it every time I pass your office. I want to steal it."

"I think it's one of my best palette knife paintings, it has some of my best spontaneity, although Tom James calls it 'Robert Randall's kindergarten painting.'"

"I've just been canned, I want to buy it before I leave."

"You've been what?"

"Yeah, Tom James, of all people, had me fired, today."

"Tom James, why?"

"I confronted him in a meeting this morning, and when the client agreed with me instead of him, he fired me on the spot."

"What's going on with Tom James?"

"I don't know, I just know I'll never have to deal with him again."

"I wish I could say that."

"Bob, how much do you want for 'Montauk Point?'"

"$450.00."

"Sold, here's fifty bucks," he reaches into his pocket and pulls out two wrinkled twenties and a ripped ten."

"What about the rest?"

"I'll pay you over the next two months."

He reaches up, grabs the painting from the wall, and zips out the door.

When I call him at his new agency the following week, they say he has been fired from there, too.

I never see another penny of the remaining $400.00.

I was fast-talked by the king of fast-talkers.

But in the end, I got even. I hadn't signed the painting; I told Bradley I would sign it after he made the last payment. And after all, he did end up stealing the painting from me.

Running the gauntlet

Now I'm at the agency on "Gauntlet Day." It was my job to interview some of the most beautiful lingerie models in the world. It's a tough job, but somebody's got to do it.

One of my assignments at DDBO is to create ads for the Hydra Fibers account, and one of their fibers is Hydrex, a synthetic, stretch fiber used to make women's bras and girdles. The Hydra ads feature the names of the cutter mills that use the fiber to make bras and girdles, giving them free ad exposure in direct relationship to the volume of fiber they buy. It's an elaborate kickback scheme.

I have to design and produce these print ads, which include choosing and hiring the lingerie models.

The tricky part is in having to design the ads with three logos, the fiber manufacturer, the name of the fabric and the name of the cutter mill.

Today, I'm interviewing fashion models from all the top model agencies in the city. This is a big project so every model agency in the city demands to have their models included in the review. The DDBO art directors all delightfully approve, the more models the merrier. Mind you now, every model must not only be a great looking girl, she has to be able fill out the 36-C sample bras that the cutters supply.

"Okay, send in the first one," I tell the receptionist out by the elevators on the phone. The girls have been gathering for about a half hour.

The lobby gets to be bedlam on this day that I'm interviewing the bra models. The word sweeps throughout the agency over what is known as the "Tit Grapevine," that this is "Gauntlet Day." The day the models have to walk the gauntlet to my office from the reception room.

Virtually every man in the agency takes a tour of the 12th floor art department lobby at least twice before the models start their trepid march to my office. They even make up excuses to be in the art department today.

The distance from the lobby to my office is down one short corridor and a right turn down a second long corridor, altogether, about a three to four hundred feet promenade in total. Each model must make this trek carrying their photo portfolios past all the art directors in the department. From the second they start this arduous journey, all hell breaks loose, every art director starts to howl catcalls and yell and scream vile sounds accompanied by the sound of metal rulers clanking on the water bowls they each have on their taborets. By the time the model is halfway to my office, the noise reaches a deafening crescendo.

I think back to the days when I was out in the cubicles, banging away on my water bowl and screeching and screaming. Each and every model has their own unique walking style, with their heels clicking away on the glistening, green Armstrong linoleum tiles as they glide along in their tight skirts and snug-fitting blouses toting their black portfolios at their side. Some try to walk fast with their breasts excessively jiggling in tempo with their gait. Others go slowly trying to attract as much attention as possible, hoping the increased volume of noise will affect my decision to use them.

The lecherous "Spike Jones" symphony lasts a full 5-minutes for each model, until their crimson faces arrive in my doorway. Many of my fellow art directors abruptly barge into my office in hopes of seeing a model trying on one of the bras. The more I try to stop them the more they continue. The interesting part is that I am required to have a woman copywriter present at all times, because the models will occasionally be standing topless in my office. The situation is so bad that some of the art directors go to the building across the street from my office to leer at the models with binoculars. I simply close the blinds, shut. They are pissed at me, and they'll be doing all sorts of things to get even with me over the next week.

I interviewed over thirty girls today. I am exhausted by the time I see the last one at 6 p.m. It's a lot of hard work. That's my story, and I'm going to stick to it.

Tom James is so jealous, he has tried several times to get me taken off the account, but fortunately, the client likes me better than him.

Don Gordon, the client, told Tom James point blank, "You take Bob Randall off my account and I'll fire your agency's ass."

That only made things worse between Tom James and me.

Carl Lecher alias Clark Kent

Now, through my office door comes the new tech writer, Carl Lecher. He's been assigned to write for the industrial division of the DuPont account. The first time I saw him it hit me how much he looks like Clark Kent. He could not look more like Clark Kent than if Joe Shuster had drawn him himself. He has a pronounced square jaw, dark slick-back hair and black horn-rimmed glasses with his muscles bulging under a sleek blue-surge suit.

"Hi, Carl, what can I do for you?"

"I wanted to talk about a new DuPont ad."

"Oh, good, sit down."

Over the last 2-years we've worked together on several ads for DuPont industrial products. One is "Ludox." Would you believe it's a chemical product that they developed for coating corrugated cardboard cartons to prevent them from sliding off one another when they are stacked high on a shipping palette."

As Carl described it in his headline, "Ludox has True Grit." It is actually made from sand infused in a chemical base that is coated on cardboard during production to keep tall stacks of cartons from slipping off one another and falling down causing possible injury to the workers who move the skids of cartons, as well as, preventing damage to whatever's inside. During the time I've worked with Carl I have learned a few things about him. His mother always calls him "Carlheinz," blending his first and middle names together into one name. He didn't like it much, but he loves his mother so much he just tolerates it. His last name is a misnomer; he is anything but a "lecher." Carl is one of the sweetest, most caring and generous people on the planet, always going out of his way to do good things for people. He once gave some of his vacation time to a writer who needed to go to Florida to visit a dying sibling. But he wasn't immune from having a run-in with Tom James. Tom called Carl to his office one day, to berate him for not getting his approval on an ad he had written for DuPont. Carl straightened him out in quick order, he told him that the client loved the copy and he didn't care what Tom thought as long as the client liked it. Tom did his usual number about being the boss and being able to fire him any time he wanted to. Carl stood up, stepped right into Tom's face and said, "Your messing with the wrong guy. You fire me and you're a dead man." Tom James never bothered him again; in fact, he avoided Carl at all cost. I thought many times about trying Carl's tactic, but I never had the guts.

Raunchy trip to Nassau

Next, it's a cold February day and I'm at the agency.

There is a standing joke in the DDBO Creative Department, in all creative departments for that matter, that when an art director wants to take a nice warm vacation, especially in the wintertime, he simply draws palm trees and sandy beaches in his layouts or TV storyboards, thus requiring a location shooting somewhere in a warmer climate. I'm no dummy I had caught on to the ruse pretty quickly.

It's the middle of this freaking, freezing-cold February, the sky is dark and the snow is falling down outside my window in big wet globs and I'm busy drawing palm trees and sandy beaches into all my layouts and hearing calypso music in my ears. It's my only hope of getting out of here to someplace warm. The collection of samples of men's summer fashions for the Hydra Fibers account is piling up in my office. Messengers from all over the garment district down on Seventh Avenue are streaming in and out of my office endlessly hanging plastic garment bags with sample men's jackets, slacks, suits and sweaters on the pipe rack in the corner of my office.

The client has approved the tropical layouts, so we all anxiously begin to plan on producing them in a tropical setting.

The process starts by selecting a photographer and then interviewing models for the succulently juicy trip to a warm climate. We not only need male models but female models also to model the several pieces of women's clothing that the client arranged to be featured in the ads also. It's an exchange deal the kind that most clients work out with other compatible manufacturers.

This trip promises to be one of the most insane trips I have ever taken. Dick Martin, one of the art directors in my group is begging to go along. He is an absolute madman, a star performer at the annual day-before- Christmas celebration and the company outing. He has a reputation for doing outrageously stupid things.

Of course, we decide that it is necessary for us to go down to Nassau, in the Bahamas, for just the right weather and visual backgrounds. Dick has been drawing palm trees into his layouts also.

My first choice of photographer is Richard Avelon, but unfortunately, he's not available. And besides, I don't think the budget could handle it.

So I pick up the phone, "Marilyn, is Phil there? It's Bob Randall of DDBO...yes, thank you."

"Bob, old buddy, how are you?" Phil Robinson's voice, my second choice photographer, comes out of my phone.

"I'm fine. I have a question for you, Phil. How would you like to spend a week in Nassau?"

"Nassau County on Long Island?"

"No, Nassau in the Bahamas."

"When do we leave?"

"Next week, if you're available."

"Trust me, I'm available, I'll rearrange my schedule to be there. I could use some warmth in my life right now."

"When can we meet to go over it, Phil?"

"Are you free for lunch, today?"

"Yes."

"Let's meet at '21'"

"'21,' that's one of the most expensive restaurants in the city, isn't it?"

"Bob, you're now worth it."

"What time?"

"How's 12:30?"

"This'll be great, my chance to actually have lunch at '21'"

"You'll love it, it's one of the most famous 'watering holes' in the city. It was founded as a speakeasy during Prohibition, in the1920's, by two cousins Jack Kriendler and Charlie Berns. They had an ingenious system of ropes and pulleys that could dispose of all the booze in minutes down a secret chute and into the New York City sewer system every time the cops and FBI raided the place."

"Where is it located?"

"It's up an 52nd Street, number 21 West, just off 5th Avenue. Look for the small, colorful statues of jockeys in front of the wrought-iron, New Orleans style facade."

"I'll see you there at 12:30."

I get there first and wait in the lobby; Phil comes strolling through the door.

"Hello, Mr. Robinson, right this way, your usual table is waiting."

"Usual table?" How impressive, I think.

"Bob, I'm excited about our trip, I've never been to Nassau."

"Neither have I. We have Larry Beal to thank, he told the client the photography for the new spring clothing had to be shot in a warm tropical climate because the ads are running in the summer time."

"Here's to Larry Watson. Let's order. Have you ever tried the '21 Raw-Bar?' Raw oysters and clams on the half-shell?"

"No."

"21 is world-famous for their raw bar, you've got to have some."

"Okay. I'll give them a try."

"Wilfred, we're ready for two Beefeater martinis straight up with a twist and two raw bar specials."

"No Phil, I prefer milk."

"Okay, milk it is, Wilfred."

Within what seemed to be seconds, Phil's martini and my milk land on the table in front of us. They are both in gigantic martini glasses. We chuckle.

Phil ceremoniously raises his glass high in the air, "Here's to our escapade to the Bahamas."

The images I drew into my layouts become vividly photographic.

Now, the steel band's Calypso music is wafting through the warm tropical air as we arrive at the luxurious beachfront hotel just outside the city of Nassau, near the bridge to "Paradise Island," giving me a heightened anticipation of exciting things to happen. I'm praying I won't be disappointed.

I decide to have my first on-location meeting with Phil Robinson and his crew in the hotel bar, to workout the schedule of shooting for the week.

It is nearly 9:00 p.m. and we are sitting at the bar in the hotel lounge. There is a huge fish tank in the center of the bar. Suddenly right before our eyes three of the models that are traveling with us appear in the tank, and they are naked. Bubbles are streaming off their slender bodies.

It seems so surreal. It dawns on me that what looks like a big fish tank behind the bar is actually the hotel swimming pool. The models obviously don't know that either. What must seem like a mirror to them under water at this end of the pool is, in fact, a window that looks into the pool from the bar. The lounge is so dark the swimmers obviously can't see us, but we can see them because the pool is lighted. And we all like what we are seeing.

Within a minute everyone in the lounge crowds in around us at the bar. Even the bartender gets in on the act; he picks up the phone at the other end of the bar and calls some of his buddies, "Hey, you guys, get your butts over here quick."

As I check out the models floundering around in the water, I'm shocked to see two dark, native boys join them in the water, their soft private parts swing back and forth with the action of the water as they become firmer and firmer. In minutes the lounge is bedlam; everyone is yelling and screaming as the couples come closer to the window, their naked bodies at times actually touching the glass. It's obvious they can't hear us. The native boys, now fully aroused, begin to chase the models around the pool. They try to engage in intercourse, but the water doesn't cooperate in the process, the more forcefully they push the more the girls are moved away in the water. After about 5-minutes of valiant trying, and much to our dismay, the young men seem to give up and disappear from the pool.

The mob in the lounge simultaneously rushes to the stairway and up to the pool deck to confront the models in person.

There they are, standing bare-naked huddled on the deck by the lounge chairs, scrambling to get dressed while the natives are back and attempting to finish what they started in the pool. But as soon as they see us, the girl's scream and run for cover and the boys scram.

Two nights later, a very inebriated Dick Martin, decides to pull one of his maniac maneuvers.

As we come out of one of the fancy downtown Nassau restaurants, called the 'Junk Canoe,' we hail a cab to take us back to the hotel. It's 2 a.m., the streets are deserted, and there's just one cab available, but it only holds 6 persons and we have 7, so Dick decides to climb up onto the roof of the taxi for the ride back to the hotel.

Mind you, we're now in the center of downtown Nassau.

He yells, "Let's get the hell out of here before the cops come." We can see Dick's fingers clutching the inside edge of the frame of the two open front windows on each side of the cab, holding on for dear life, as the taxi takes us back to the hotel with him yelling and screaming at the top of his lungs all the way.

When we get to the hotel I go right to bed, I'm tired from the trip. I know that in the morning I'll have to be ready to begin the scouting and selection of locations at 8 a.m.

I had brushed my teeth, turned out the light and gotten into bed when Dick, who I'm sharing the room with, comes in. It's now past 3 a.m. We have to share a room it's part of the client's budget rules. This room happens to have a king size bed which we both are forced to share. I'm almost asleep and the room is totally dark. I hear him undress and get into bed. Then I feel another body get into the bed with us, it is obviously a native hooker that Dick had just picked up outside the hotel. He begins to have sex with her. I come rousing out of my semi sleep state and say: "Hey, what the hell is going on here, Dick?"

"I'm getting laid," is his drunken remark, "you can be next."

"I don't want to be next," I yell, seeing in the dark that he is on top of a beautiful Island girl, her teeth glistening in a ray of light that is streaming in from the slightly ajar bathroom door. Her strong Island perfume is almost suffocating me.

"You can be next, mon," she says, "I only charge you twenty dollars."

"I don't want to be next," I respond indignantly, rolling over, trying to go back to sleep.

The two of them go on for what seems like an hour, but I'm sure it's only a few minutes.

"Want to be next?" she asks me again, tapping me on the shoulder.

"I just want you to leave, now, before I call the front desk."

She jumps to her feet, pulls her dress over her head and races out of the room, in a flash.

"Your out of your mind, Dick," I say to my friend.

All I get for a response is a loud drunken snore. He's asleep already.

The next morning I meet up with the Phil and stylist on the deck next to the pool. There is a breakfast buffet under the thatched umbrella for us to enjoy. One of the swimming models from the other night, a Janet Mullaney, is sitting on one of the lounge chairs with a plate of food resting on her beautiful knees.

"Good morning, Robert," she cheerfully says. "What did you do last night, I missed you at the bar."

I just couldn't tell her what happened in our room I'm too embarrassed. And I certainly am not going to tell her I was ogling her from the lounge.

I just know that the advertising business is proving to be more and more mad.

My involuntary interlude continues

My mind suddenly tries to focus on the here and now. How long have I been suspended in this flashback mode? This must be what it's like when you die and your whole life passes before your eyes. But I have mostly been seeing the bad things not the good. Has it been minutes or hours? My nature,is to be calm and patient, but right now I am inordinately anxious. My senses tell me I'm still standing in Thom James' office and the somewhat fuzzy image of Thom James' body on the floor next to me is invading my flash back thoughts. I must be in some kind of self-induced hypnotic trance.

I start to hear the sounds of the "White Horse Club" marching into my brain pushing reality out, again.

Threats at the Greenbrier

"Mr. Randall, there's a call for you." The tall, slim, Negro waiter, decked-out in a spotless white jacket, announces as he approaches our table. Negro's can be servants but they still can't stay here at the famous Greenbrier Resort in West Virginia. I'm down here with Phil Newton, the account supervisor on the New England Banker's Association account, and his wife Sharon and my wife Jean. I was able to fly us all down in my twin-engine plane, 4375P. We first had to stopover in New York so Phil and I could attend a Plans Review Board meeting for the Meriweather Computer account, one of Boston's most important clients. We're here attending a special annual meeting of the New England Banker's Association, relaxing from the flight in the equestrian-styled "White Horse Club."

"So this is the famous Greenbrier. I like it. It has great charm and southern elegance. I just love the cozy cabin we're in," Sharon says.

"I'm glad I could get a chance to be here," Jean adds.

Because the area where the resort is located is a "dry" area, they've created the White Horse Club as a private club where they can serve alcohol to its members. So, all you have to do is pay a dollar to join and then you can have all the booze you want. It is their clever way of getting around the law.

"Can I take the call here?"

"No sir, you have to go back to your room to get the call. Just pick up your phone and ask the operator for your call."

"Thanks." I get up and start to move as fast as possible back to my room; I'm worried that there could be some kind of emergency back home. Who knows, other than family, that I'm here? I think.

"I'll go with you," Phil says."

When we get to the room, I pick up the phone, "May I help you?" the operator says.

"I'm Robert Randall, I understand that you have a call for me?"

"Yes, hang up and I will put it through to you."

"R-i-n-g."

"Robert Randall."

"Randall your ass is in deep shit, your Plans Review Board meeting this morning for the Meriweather Computer account was a total disaster. None of the board members liked the campaign you presented. I want you to get your ass back here to the New York office tonight, to rework it," an angry Tom James' voice comes booming out of the receiver.

"Tonight?"

"Yeah, that's what I said, tonight."

"But we're down here attending a special annual client meeting of New England Banker's Association."

"I don't care whose meeting you're attending, you're not going to spend any time tonight enjoying yourself at the Greenbrier while I'm up here working my ass off."

"Tom, I'm here with Phil Newton, the account supervisor on the account."

"I don't care who you're with, I'm in charge of creative for the whole agency and I want you back here immediately."

"Hold on, Phil Newton wants to talk to you."

"I don't want to talk to him."

I hand the phone to Phil, anyway.

"Tom, this is Phil Newton..."

"I want Randall back here tonight."

"That's not possible, Tom, we flew down in Bob's plane and he won't be able to get a clearance out of here tonight, the weather is foggy and we're socked-in. And besides, the client is expecting Bob to make a presentation of next year's advertising campaign to all the members of the association in about an hour."

"Put Randall on."

"Randall, you've got a reprieve for now. I want you here in the New York office first thing on Monday. And this moves you to the top of my shit list."

"Click," Tom James hangs up.

It is still incredibly difficult to figure out what makes Tom James tick. Perhaps we'll never know. One of the elements in our relationship is that he is afraid to fly and I own my own plane.

Freud said, *"On the basis of clinical evidence we can suppose that paranoics are endowed with a fixation at the stage of narcissism, and we can assert that the amount of regression characteristic of paranoia is indicated by the length of the step from sublimated homosexuality to narcissism."*

It turns out the Plans Review Board only have a couple of minor suggestions; they actually liked the ads I had presented.

One good thing, almost

Up pops the only time that my brain can remember when Tom James' insanity resulted in something positive happening for the agency. I had written a theme line for one of the accounts in the Boston office, the Ollie Tool Company. The theme is: "The tools that father's will to sons." It's based on research that said Ollie's tools are better made and outlasted the competition by a wide margin; a significant quality story. Of course, as required, I have to first present the campaign idea along with the theme line, storyboards and layouts to the Creative Plans Review Board in the New York office of DDBO. This time Tom James is in the meeting. I present the campaign and theme line to the board. The members of the Plans review Board didn't much like the theme. "Robert, we think you can do better than that," one of them says.

"It's my line," interrupts, Tom James, "I wrote it. It's better than anything the losers in the Boston office could ever come up with," he gloats.

"Tom?" is all I can say, knowing that I wrote the line.

"Randall, I want you to take my theme line back to the client and sell it."

"Whatever you say, Tom, you're the boss."

I'm not sure what Tom has up his sleeve. Did he take credit for my line thinking that would impress the board and get them to agree to let me present it to the client? No one ever knows what Tom has up his sleeve.

We go back to Boston to arrange a meeting with the Ollie Tool Company to present the campaign. I wasn't in the office more than 10-minutes when the phone rings.

"Randall, if you don't sell my theme line to the Ollie Tool Company, start looking for a new job."

"Tom, it's not your theme line and you know it. It's my line."

"You just sell my line to them or you're dead."

"Click."

The next morning I take the campaign to the client.

I first present the research findings that led to our conclusion to write the line. Then I show them the new theme line. They say they understand the rationale behind it but they just don't like it.

"It just doesn't hit us," the advertising manager, Jim Crandall, says, "why don't you go back and give it another try."

"The agency believes this is the right theme line for you, Jim."

"Give it another try, Bob."

We leave, very disappointed.

When I get back to the office, I call Tom James. "Tom, they didn't buy the theme line."

"What? You march your ass right back there and do anything you have to do to convince them that that theme line is perfect for them, anything."

"But they don't like it."

"Let's put it this way, Randall, if you don't sell them my theme line your paycheck stops."

Ordinarily I wouldn't be concerned by someone threatening me, but in this case, Tom James has an ugly track record for delivering on his threats; he's had over 30-people fired since he became world wide creative director, so I know he isn't kidding. And after all it is my theme line.

The next morning I call the client and tell them I want to discuss the new advertising campaign.

When I walk into the client's office, Jim Crandall stands up and says: "That was fast, let's see the new campaign approach, Robert."

I smile and suggest he sit down. Jim Crandall is a soft-spoken man with a slicked-back hairstyle wearing both suspenders and a belt, a very cautious person. The domineering owners of the company have made him that way.

I reach down and pull the layouts from the black portfolio at my side. I hold them tight to my chest so he can't see that they, in fact, are the exact same layouts I presented yesterday. As I begin my presentation, I realize that I'm keeping them clutched so tight that my fingers are turning white.

Jim slides forward in his chair, a broad smile of anticipation spanning his face.

"Arum." I clear my throat as I begin, "Jim, DDBO and the Ollie Tool Company have enjoyed a long, mutually beneficial relationship. The Ollie Tool Company is one of DDBO's very first clients. Back to before it even became DDBO. If ever the agency would consider resigning your account, we are at the very edge of that precipice today."

Jim pulls back in his chair, folding his arms uncomfortably.

"The agency feels so strongly about this theme line that if you don't agree to use it I have been authorized to resign your account effective immediately."

I slowly, ever so slowly, turn the layout around to reveal the exact same design and theme line I had presented the day before.

"Ollie Tools. The tools that fathers will to sons."

Jim's eyes are now bigger than dinner plates as he starts to stutter, squirming as if his butt is wedged between a rock and a hard place. "Well…er…well…er…er…Robert…err…I didn't know that you and the agency felt that strongly about the theme line. Why of course then, by all means, let's go ahead and use it."

I don't know who was more relieved, Jim or I.

I called Tom James from the client's reception room and told him of the Ollie Tool Company decision.

"See, I told you they would buy my line, asshole."

At the next DDBO convention at the Roosevelt Hotel, Tom James showed the ad and took credit for the theme line. I really don't know if he had some sick thought that he actually wrote the line himself. I'm sure Freud would have a lot to say about it.

Debauchery at Montauk Point

Now I'm seeing Jack Baron the General Brands account executive pleading with me, "Come on Bob you've got to volunteer to go, we need you there, nobody else can do it, you're the fastest art director DDBO has."

I know it's the agency's only chance to make a bundle signing up the liquor storeowners and distributors for upcoming advertising campaigns.

"I can't Jack, I just got married and I don't spend enough time with Jean as it is. And with those Global Broadcasting tune-in ads I have to work late almost every night. I never have time to go home. And who wants to go to a dumb sales meeting at Montauk Point in the middle of the winter?"

"It's your chance to make them some extra cash. The agency will give you a nice bonus if you'll go. You're the only art director who knows how to please that nut Larry Ryan."

"Bonus, how much?"

Suddenly my mind starts seeing all the reasons we could use a few extra dollars.

"$500."

"$500? Are you serious?"

"That's nothing to sneeze at, Bob."

"We can really use the money. But tomorrow's Friday."

"That's right, we want to get there early so we can schmooze with all the client's buyers as they arrive in the afternoon. Tell your wife your going to make $500 for two days work, that'll shut her up."

"I have to get these Global Broadcasting ads done, they're due tomorrow."

"Don't worry, I'll get Svenson to do them."

"He'll be upset with me."

"Don't you worry about it, I'll tell him he'll have to go if he doesn't let you go. I outrank him, he'll do it."

"What time do we have to leave?"

"6 a.m."

"6 a.m.?"

"Yeah, it's over a 3-hour drive to Montauk Point. I'll pick you up at 6 in front of the office. Be ready, pack your bag tonight."

"6 a.m.?"

"Don't worry, Tom James is going to be there, you'll be able to make some "brownie points" with him."

"But I want to stay as far away as possible from him."

"Okay, suit yourself."

"But I live out on the Island. Can't you pick me up at my house, it's on the way?"

"Okay, if that's what it's going to take to get you to go. I'll be there at 7 a.m. sharp."

The next morning at 6:30 a.m., Jack Baron is sitting in his car in front of our apartment, beeping the horn. I race down the stairs and out to the curb waving my arms to get him to stop with the horn. I load up my layout supplies, kiss Jean goodbye, and we're on our way.

After a boring three and a half hour ride out through the Hamptons and Amagansett, the sight of what resembles a giant medieval castle appears on the horizon. The surrounding area is cold and bleak looking, totally deserted. Barren sand dunes covered with tall waving sea grass and snow fences stretch for miles in all directions. A few hundred screeching sea gulls circle in the clear but blustery blue sky above. It's like a scene out of an Agatha Christie mystery story.

As we approach Montauk Manor, I can see the parking area is packed with cars and General Brands trucks. The drivers dolly case after case of liquor into the hotel.

"Bob, let's check in and then we'll go and find the client."

"Sounds good to me. Do I have time to get a cup of coffee?"

"Absolutely, but don't forget your layout pads, pencils and pastels. You've got work to do."

The inside of the castle looks pretty much like the outside, with towering red brick walls. Only there are dozens of glittering suits of armor lined up against them. The lobby is crowded with surly-looking liquor storeowners and dozens of bartenders. Most of them are here for the fun. Sprinkled among them is a selection of New York City's choice hookers. Brought out here at great expense, to service liquor storeowners and bartenders. But there's no sign of Hercule Poriot the Belgian detective, who has been lurking about in my mind.

As we pass the Grand Ballroom we can see the crews setting up the booths and displays. Jack gestures for us to enter as he gives me a guided tour of the ballroom and the rationale behind these meetings.

"This is where the General Brands sales staff will be signing up the buyers. The more they buy the more they get in hookers and cash. It's all done surreptitiously, away from the prying eyes of the IRS and the law.

It's the main reason they hold these 'sales meetings' in this desolate town of Montauk Point, one hundred and fifty miles from New York City, in the dead middle of the winter. Nobody knows what's going on out here. And in the wintertime you can spot a cop or a Fed a mile away."

"Jack, you sure know a lot about the mentality of these guys."

"Bob, let's grab that cup of coffee and go up to our room to get it set up so you can start cranking out those layouts for the buyers. I'll check-in and get the keys and meet you at the elevators."

The arrangement is, the owners and dealers get so many dollars in ads for so many cases of liquor that they buy. They call it "co-op advertising" but it's really a legalized way to deliver kick back's to the buyers, owners and bartenders. The General Brands sales force gives the buyers a sales receipt that Jack Baron translates into ad space. He gives me the size the ad should be for each buyer and I create the ad, doing a layout with the brands the owners and dealers have agreed to feature in the ad with their individual store names and logos. By having everyone here in one place, General Brands and DDBO can get them all signed up in one place in two days, otherwise, it would take many months and all the time and expense of running all over the country to meet with these guys. Within hours the ad requests start to stream in, slowly at first, then they begin to pile up.

I just keep knocking out the layouts. The day wears on layout after layout. The clients sign off on the ads as I get them completed. Jack keeps a detailed list for the DDBO billing department. Throughout the day he brings me food to keep me going, he doesn't want me to stop for a second.

At one point I go into the bathroom, it's freezing in here, someone left the window open. As I'm standing there I hear voices coming in the open window. I go to the window and see that it's a casement type window that is cranked open. As I start to crank it closed to keep out the cold, I realize not only can I hear what they are saying in the next room, I can see images of the people also, reflected in our window which is lined up exactly with their window. They are at precisely the same 45-degree angle. Geometry was one of my favorite subjects in high school.

"Hello 'Mr. Smith,' I'm Trixie." Their conversation bounces off their window hits our window and comes in.

"Well, hell-ohh Trixie."

"That will be one hundred dollars, 'Mr. Smith.'"

"We've got it covered, Trixie," says another voice. I think it's one of the General Brands sales guys.

In the reflections I can see a salesman sitting in a chair with his back to their bathroom, but I can't see the other man. Suddenly, a sexy looking woman, with a tight skirt and big boobs comes into view. She takes the man's hand and disappears out of sight. "Right this way, big boy."

"Enjoy, 'Mr. Smith,'" a third voice says.

I hear what must be a bedroom door close, apparently leaving the two men alone in the room.

"He knows too much, we may have to get rid of him," I hear the first man whisper.

"We can't do that, it's too risky," the third man quietly responds.

"We have to, there's too much at stake, we could lose it all," the unseen man says.

"Let's not talk about it here, let's talk about it when we get back to the City." he cautions, in a whisper.

I hear the room door open and close as he exits, I slowly crank the window closed. I'm tempted to go to the door to see who this guy is but that's too risky. I'm beginning to realize just how dangerous these people are. I wonder what bizarre kinds of things are going on in all the other rooms in the hotel.

One of the nicest parts of being up here away from the crowd is not having to deal with Tom James. I wonder what he is doing?

Jack returns.

"You know what I just heard, Jack?"

"What?"

I heard two men in the room next door plotting to get rid of someone."

"Probably just firing one of the distributors, it happens all the time."

"It sounded much more sinister than that. They also paid for a hooker for some guy."

"Bob, this is your first General Brands sales meeting, if you want to keep your job, one thing you've got to learn is to 'See no evil, hear no evil and speak no evil.'"

Getting Even

"Good morning, Bob-O," the voice on the phone says, "it's Sandy, I want you to be one of the first to know that I have accepted the position of Director of Marketing at, of all places, Norman Cosmetics."

"Wow."

"I started this morning."

"That sounds great, Sandy"

"Bob-O, I want to ask a favor of you. Can you come up to my office to discuss the tune-in ads for 'The Big Money Question?' I have some ideas on how we can improve them."

"Sure, should we tell my boss about our meeting?"

"I already spoke to Sven, I've invited him too, you may want to share a cab with him. I have also ordered Tom James to put in an appearance; I just want to straighten him out on one thing. I think you might find it interesting."

I dial the phone, "Sven, did you get a call from Sandy Burnstein?"

"Yes, I did. Very interesting, I think we better get going."

"What about Tom James?"

"I spoke to him, he wants to go separately."

"Sandy said he wanted to discuss 'The Big Money Question' tune-in ads."

"I have a hunch he's going to discuss more than that Bob."

"All right driver, we'll get out here."

We enter the building and go up to Norman Cosmetics on the 5th floor. Tom James is already there. He doesn't say a word to us. He just sits staring into space, rotating his fingertips on the side table like a racehorse rounding the turn.

"Hello, Mr. Randall and Mr. Svenson, Mr. Burnstein will see all of you shortly," the receptionist greets us.

Tom's face is steaming, he is furious at being ordered to this meeting where we have also been invited.

"Tell Sandy I don't have much time," Tom barks.

"He'll be with you shortly, Mr. James."

The receptionist gets up and walks to the office on the far wall opposite Mr. Norman's office and opens the door.

"Follow me, please."

We enter and Sandy is sitting at his desk writing.

"Hello, Bob, Sven, Tom, please sit down."

"What the hell is this all about, Sandy?" Tom demands.

"Tom, I want to discuss the tune-in ads for 'The Big Money Question' TV show. I want…"

"What about them?" Tom interrupts.

"Excuse me Tom, I want you to know that I have decided to have Bob Randall handle the tune-in advertising for 'The Big Money Question' TV show."

"I'll decide that, not you."

"Tom, there's no secret you and I haven't gotten along very well, so I'm going to make it very clear, either 'Bob-O,' here handles the Big Money Question ads or I move the whole Norman Cosmetics account to Y&R with Bob."

Tom stands up, doesn't say a word and storms out of Sandy's office.

"'Bob-O,' if he gives you any trouble on this, you let me know. I think he now knows exactly where I stand with his pathetic attitude."

Sven reaches over and shakes my hand, "Congratulations, Bob, you've done a great job; I'll let Harry Beal know of Sandy's decision."

The ANDY Awards

The noise level is as high as the mouthwatering aroma level of the sizzling filet mignons that the waiters are delivering to the tables throughout the ballroom of the Waldorf Astoria Hotel. It's crowded with all the creative luminaries of the New York advertising scene. This event is the first ANDY Awards, a competition to honor creativity in advertising throughout the world, sponsored by The Advertising Club of New York.

One of the members of the awards committee had called me yesterday and asked if I was planning to attend. Even though we had submitted entries, I said I wasn't. The woman on the phone said that our entry was a finalist in its category and I might want to plan to attend.

"Did I win?"

"I can't tell you that, but it might be wise for you to be here. DDBO has a table."

"I'll be there."

I could see the sign on the center of the table toward the back of the room it read "DDBO." I headed for it.

As I approached, Tom James spotted me. "What are you doing here, Randall?"

"The awards committee called yesterday and asked me to be here."

"Your not sitting at this table, go find somewhere else to sit."

"Over here, Bob" the voice of Lenny Kravitz, the creative director of Arnold and Company, another Boston advertising agency, comes looming from behind me. The advertising community in Boston is much friendlier than New York. Back when Lenny first learned that I was going to Boston to take over DDBO's art department, he arranged to meet me at a New York photographer's studio to extend me his own personal welcome to Boston.

"Don't let Tom James bother you, he did the same to your predecessor."

"Oh, he did?"

"Come on, have lunch with us."

After the lunch, the waiters remove all the dishes and the festivities begin — non other than Johnny Carson's sidekick, Ed McMahon, is the master of ceremonies. Over the next hour, dozens of creative types parade to the podium to collect their statues.

Then they come to the trade ad category: "And the ANDY Award for the world's best trade ad goes to Robert Randall, the creative director of the Boston office of DDBO." As I stand up to go and get my statue, Lenny says, "Great job, Bob, that ad you did for the Westbrook Paper Company is outstanding, and your ANDY Award is the only one DDBO got today. You should be very proud."

"Thanks, Lenny."

When I get to the podium, Ed McMahon hands me the statue. It weighs a ton; it's an 18-inch tall gold sculpture of a man blowing a heraldic horn. On my way back to the table I pass the DDBO table. Everyone is applauding except Tom James. He's just puffing on his cigar with an angry look of complete hatred on his face.

"You guys want to have a drink with me to celebrate?"

"Nobody at this table is going to have a drink with you, Randall, they have to get back to work and you have to get your ass back to Boston."

I ignore him.

"I'll have a drink with you," Lenny says.

I turn to leave with Lenny and I look back at Tom James, all I can think of is something that Freud once said, *"We may suppose that the final aim of the destructive instinct is to reduce things to an inorganic state. For this reason we also call it the 'death instinct."*

"You're fired!"

My brain is now recalling today's meeting.

The five o'clock "emergency" meeting is about to start in the eleventh-floor corner office of DDBO President and Chief Executive Officer, Harold Beal. The office overlooks Madison Avenue, one of the most famous streets in the world. Many psychiatrists refer to it as the "Avenue of Madness."

The usual collection of "brown noses" are already helping themselves to drinks at the president's lavish bar in the corner of the room. It's the middle of July and the outside temperature is over 96 degrees. The meeting has been hastily called to present new television ideas to one of the agency's largest, most demanding clients, the Regal Hotel chain. The chain, which is headquartered in Boston, had recently been taken over by the giant multi-national ITC, International Tech Corporation. After the takeover, ITC's CEO, Phillip "Killer" Roberts, made no secret about the fact that he hated the present advertising campaign that was running for Regal Hotels. He had sent a scathing memo from Europe to George Elliott, the ITC International Director of Marketing, demanding that the "stupid ads, with the little girl smiling," be changed immediately. "Our target audience is business travelers, not grinning babies," the memo read. He ordered that the replacement storyboards be ready for him to review the morning after his private jet lands at LaGuardia Airport. And that is tomorrow morning.

This is why the emergency meeting was called and why we are all here.

It is now approaching 5:20 p.m. and all the invited participants have arrived. Attending, are all the key players on the account both from the Boston office of DDBO, where the account is handled, and all the top brass in the New York office, along with the client's marketing guys at Regal Hotel, who were in power before the recent takeover. Plus all the top marketing and advertising guys from ITC's Park Avenue headquarters in New York City are here. It was a hostile takeover, so a thick animosity-laden, overly patronizing dialog fills the room like Jell-O, oozing into every tiny crack and crevice in the room.

The four-man ITC contingent, headed by George Elliott, take up positions on the soft couches along the right-hand wall of Harold Beal's office.

The Regal Hotel participants from Boston, consist of the Worldwide Director of Marketing and Sales, Bob Winters, and the Director of Marketing and Advertising, Morton Williams. They grab the chairs directly in front of the president's desk. Mr. Beal, the chubby and ever-charming president of DDBO, is, of course, seated behind that Early American style white pine desk which he has strategically positioned at an angle between the two huge corner windows, turning his back on Madison Avenue. He has a gigantic Cuban cigar protruding from the corner of his mouth. He's from the mid-west where his family owns and runs one of the biggest regional dairy farms. He was the manager of the Chicago office before he was brought to the New York office and eventually elected president. He started out as a creative guy, a copywriter.

The remainder of the New York DDBO guys is seated around the small conference table near the other window. At the head of the table, is the tall elderly Chairman of the Board, Charlie Boxer. Next to him is his protégé, and my nemesis Tom "Himself" James, the pill popping egomaniacal, Worldwide Creative Director of DDBO clutching a bundle of TV storyboards under his arm, and sweating profusely.

The DDBO Regal Hotel team from the Boston Office includes the manager of the office, Joe Haynes, the Regal Hotel Account Supervisor, Carl MacDougall, and me, Robert Randall; I'm the Creative Director of the Boston Office. We are all standing by the door because there aren't enough seats for us inside the office.

When we get back to Boston I'm sure Carl is going to catch hell from Haynes because he didn't have the brains to check the number attending to be sure there are enough chairs in the president's office, especially when Haynes himself was forced to stand by the door. It's Carl's responsibility.

We had all come down from Boston together last night on the "Owl" — the overnight train that derived its name from the fact that it leaves Boston at midnight and arrives at Grand Central Station at eight in the morning. It's a God-awful way to travel; the train makes every local stop from Boston to New York City, waking everyone on board every time it stops and starts with sudden jolts. It's referred to as the "milk run," mimicking the old days when trains would deliver fresh milk to every stop from Boston to New York City.

When the CEO of ITC had killed the Regal Hotels campaign, he ordered the spots pulled from the airwaves immediately, and all the agency commission on those national television commercials ceased, causing a major wave of panic to spread throughout the agency. Opening the door for the maniacal, Worldwide Creative Director, Tom James, to prove once again, that he is God Almighty.

He of course instantly seized the opportunity, convinced that only, he alone can come up with a solution brilliant enough to resolve the emergency situation that was threatening the loss of one of the agency's largest accounts. It was the same way that he had clawed his way to the top to become the Worldwide Creative Director of DDBO; by constantly grabbing the spotlight and taking credit for every idea that any client liked. Everyone feared him.

However, on the other hand, responding to the objections and demands that Roberts had raised in his memo, we in the Boston Office had been asked by the Regal Hotels Director of Marketing and Advertising, Morton Williams to develop our own Boston Office approach for a campaign that would replace the current award-winning campaign. We had done as he ordered and I have that campaign in a large black portfolio by my side. The Boston office contingent had spent the day rehearsing our presentation, even though now it looks like that will be an unnecessary waste of time. Because when I met Tom James in the hall before the meeting, he grabbed my arm and pulled me into one of the account executive's offices, closing the door so no one could hear what he was telling me.

"This is my meeting, Randall, you keep your mouth shut, don't say a word," he orders, his eyes stretched open like saucers and looking a little unbalanced, "...unless I tell you to."

Beal waves his hand toward the door saying: "All of you free loaders who aren't involved in this meeting, get out." Six New York office brown noses jump up and rush for the door, taking their drinks with them.

"Make sure those glasses are washed and put back in my bar before I get in, in the morning."

It is exactly 5:30 p.m., the time the air conditioning goes off in the entire building, every night. We all can hear the rush of air suddenly stop, replaced by silence. Everyone senses the temperature is about to rise. Within a minute it becomes stiflingly hot in the president's office.

Befitting his position as the senior ranking corporate officer present, ITC's Director of Marketing, George Elliot, stands up, loosens his tie and proclaims: "It's hot as hell in here. How are we going to review the creative in this heat? With all the money we're paying you, you'd think you could afford to leave the air conditioning on," he rudely adds.

Harold Beal sheepishly stands up and announces: "All right gentlemen, let's all go into the Boardroom, it has it's own air conditioner. We had it installed for our Board meetings."

"Why the hell didn't you have the meeting in there to begin with?" George Elliott snarls as he stomps out of the room with all of the ITC and Regal Hotel guys following closely behind him, almost in lockstep.

"Which way is it to the boardroom?"

"Follow me," says Joe Haynes.

The rest of us get up, and in order of our rank, march in our own style quickstep to the boardroom. When Beal enters he goes to the back corner of the room and turns on the air conditioner.

"This is more like it," George Elliott snarls again, taking his seat in the chair at the center on the long side of the table, remarking as he does: "Anywhere I sit is the head of the table."

The others all begin scrambling for seats near Mr. Elliott. As Morton Williams sits down next to him, Mr. Elliott bellows: "I want Bill Lofstead to sit here, Morton you go to the other end of the table." Clearly signaling that Morton William's future at Regal Hotels is quite possibly in doubt. Every subtle word, action and nuance has meaning and future ramifications in the advertising business.

I figure, based on Tom James' comment, it would be best for me to take a seat as far from the center of the action as I can. I keep the black portfolio at my side. The rest of the DDBO Boston contingent follows me. They all want to get as far away from him as I do. They have all had job-threatening run-ins with him over the years. Very few DDBO employees have escaped his wrath.

Mr. Beal takes the seat directly across the table from Mr. Elliott, announcing as he sits down: "We have been working hard on a new campaign for Regal Hotels. We've had our best brains, in New York, storyboarding a brilliant new approach for you."

"It better be a lot better than the last one," Mr. Elliott pronounces in a threatening tone.

"I think you're going to like what we've come up with," Beal responds as he turns to Tom James and says: "Show him what we've got, Tom."

Tom stands up and picks up the top four storyboards from the pile on the table in front of him, obnoxiously pounding them on the table as if to line them up. Everyone winces as he does so.

He begins his pitch. "We have a brilliant approach that combines both Regal Hotels and Jeeves Rent-A-Car, ITC's other company, in one 30-second commercial." Tom continues: "In the first frame, we see a businessman leaving the Jeeves Rent-A-Car counter and getting into a Jeeves Rent-a-Car at the airport. We follow him along the highway, showing beauty shots of the car, backed by dramatic music. The car finally pulls up in front of a Regal Hotel. The doorman comes out to greet our traveling businessman. The music builds to a loud crescendo. We pull back to see both the car and the hotel, as the businessman enters the hotel. We super the two logos. The announcer says: 'The Best of Both World's: Regal Hotels and Jeeves Rent-A-Car.'"

There's dead silence in the now chilly Boardroom.

Tom James sits down, taking a puff on his cigar and blowing the smoke straight up to the ceiling with a holier-than-thou look on his face.

Mr. Elliott stands up, "We can't show this to Mr. Roberts. First of all we don't know if a spot like this combining two advertisers owned by the same parent company would have any chance of passing FCC scrutiny. It's never been done before. And, the Jeeves advertising agency will be up in arms to stop it, as I'm sure you would be, if the situation was reversed."

"We think this would be breakthrough advertising, and will be well worth the fight to get it on the air. You get double the value from every spot you run," a smug, sanctimonious, Tom James asserts.

"It could take months to get the FCC's approval, and in the meantime, there would be no advertising running for Regal Hotels. It's crazy."

"Our lawyers can handle it," Mr. Beal asserts.

"What about the approach we asked for?" Mr. Elliott demands.

"We don't have any other, we really believe you should run this campaign," Tom James says, even more smugly, as if he has some power over Mr. Elliott by putting him in this, up-against-the-wall, showdown position.

"This is it, this is all you've got?" Mr. Elliott shouts.

"This is the approach we strongly recommend," Tom James says forcefully, taking a puff on his cigar now blowing the smoke across the table at Mr. Elliott in a childish show of defiance.

"We can't show this to Mr. Roberts," Mr. Elliott reaffirms, "I think it's a dumb idea."

"Show him that other approach, Tom," suggests Mr. Beal, pointing to the remaining stack of storyboards on the table in front of Tom James.

Tom lets out an audible sound of disgust; as he crushes his cigar out in the large glass ashtray in front of Mr. Elliott, visibly upset with having been forced into this position. He was trying to bully Mr. Elliot into running his dual campaign idea. A high stakes business strategy.

Tom reluctantly reaches down and picks up the remaining batch of storyboards into his hands. Again, he angrily bounces them loudly on the table. Finally holding up the first black storyboard and begins to describe the visuals sketched in each frame.

"The spot opens on a close-up of a mother's smiling face as she begins singing an original melody, created by the famous jingle writer, Mitch Henderson: 'We're happy, we're happy, we're going to a Regal Hotel.' The camera pulls back revealing her husband her daughter and her son. They are all standing in their living room, singing the same song: 'We're happy, we're happy we're going to a Regal Hotel,' Tom reads in a boring monotone voice trying to deliberately sabotage the campaign.

Before he gets to the third frame, Mr. Elliott abruptly jumps up, again. "You've got to be kidding, you're not serious you can't be. This is even worse than the campaign that we took off the air," he screams. "It's still directed to the wrong target audience. Didn't any of you imbeciles read the memo from Roberts?"

The room is as quiet as King Tut's tomb after they dropped the final huge stone slab sealing its entrance.

"It's on strategy, the husband is on a business trip and is taking his family along to have some fun." Tom feebly comments.

"What businessman in his right mind wants to take his family on a business trip with him?" screams Mr. Elliott. "That's no fun."

"We've had our best people working on it," announces Tom James.

"Well, they're not good enough," shouts Mr. Elliott.

"Do we know if Mr. Roberts jet is in the air, yet?" He spins around asking the ITC man to his right.

"I don't know," the man sheepishly answers, knowing he should have had the answer in advance. The man runs to the phone on the table next to the door of the conference room and picks up the receiver.

"Dial 9, first," advises Mr. Beal.

Everyone in the room now shifts their attention to the ITC man as he dials and waits for a response.

"It's Bill Lofstead. Do you know if Mr. Roberts' plane has left Heathrow airport?" he asks.

"It's in the air?" He continues to question the person on the other end of the phone not wanting to believe what he has just heard. "Are you sure?"

"Please check again," he presses.

"You just spoke to Mr. Roberts?" he whimpers.

The man turns and almost whispers to the entire room: "He's in the air all ready."

"What are we going to do, we can't show him any of this stuff. He'll can us all," announces Mr. Elliott.

"What the hell are we going to do?" he repeats, in desperation.

I notice a sick grin coming over Tom James's face, as if he has won and the client will have no choice but to present his dual-client campaign to Mr. Roberts.

"What are we going to do?" whines another one of the four-men in the ITC contingent, even more despairingly, obviously seeing images of his life passing in front of his eyes, confirming how overextended he is with mortgage payments, college tuition, and country club dues.

"You guys are in deep shit," yells Mr. Elliott.

The entire room has now reduced itself to the level of a bunch of little boys who have been caught doing something greatly wrong against their father, each one panicking in his own childish way. One of the ITC men is wringing his hands while another is talking to himself. "We're dead, we're dead," he repeats softly shaking his head and looking down at the table in front of him. "What are we going to do?"

It's now past 9 p.m., people are wandering around the conference table, looking almost as if they are expecting some divine answer to come thundering down through the ceiling into the room.

"Our meeting with Mr. Roberts is at 9 a.m. in the morning. Is there any way you can do something that we can show to Mr. Roberts?" asks Mr. Elliott.

"I want to show him the Jeeves-Regal campaign," Tom James pipes up with a big shit-eating grin on his face.

"Over my dead body," Mr. Elliot shouts, pounding his fist on the table.

The room reverts to total desolate silence.

"There is an answer," a timid voice comes from my left. It's Joe Haynes, General Manager of the Boston office.

"What are you talking about?" asks Charlie Boxer, DDBO Chairman.

"We have an approach to show," Joe says more forcefully.

"You do?" puzzles Charlie Boxer.

"Morton Williams had asked us to develop our own Boston Office approach to solving the problem for him," Joe informs everyone.

"That's right, I thought it would be good to have the Boston Office's ideas here also," Mr. Williams proudly declares.

"Good-God man, lets see them," pleads Mr. Elliott.

Joe turns to me and unceremoniously gives up his chair and invites me to take over the meeting to present our Boston Office idea.

I take the portfolio, which I had secretly placed under the Boardroom table next to the support leg when I came into the meeting, and step to the center of the room. I carefully remove the storyboards that my team in the Boston office had prepared under my direction.

Tom James has retreated off into the corner, visibly steaming mad.

I begin slowly; every eye in the huge conference room is now glued on me.

"Our approach deals with the businessman, our prime-target. We open the spot with a shot of a businessman getting out of a cab and entering a Regal hotel. The doorman bows, extra graciously, and opens the door for him. As he enters the lobby, a group of Regal Hotel employee's surrounds him. The sound of 'Pomp and Circumstance' begins being played in the background."

I carefully show every fame of the storyboard to each member of the Regal Hotel team.

"In Broadway Show style he is ushered up to a royal throne at the center of the lobby. A spotlight focuses on him. Next, a bellhop takes his bag. A butler puts a royal robe around his shoulders and a desk clerk places a crown on his head. The music continues, as various Hotel employees' parade by with samples of the high level of service he is about to receive. A chef spins by with a tray full of succulent food including a thick sirloin steak. A housekeeper presents wonderfully rich towels and pillows."

I point to the last frame, which is a close up of the businessman all decked out in King garb, and pause.

"A title superimposes over this last scene and the voiceover announcer, Bob Landis, says: 'At Regal Hotels you are always treated like a King.'"

"Bravo, great, sensational," shouts Mr. Elliott, with the clear tone that he appreciates that the Boston Office may have just saved everyone's jobs. "It's perfect, right on the money," he adds.

"I knew the boys in the Boston Office could do it," Mr. Williams says with pride. He reaches over and shakes my hand. "Great job, Randall."

"I've got to get going, I'm late for an important dinner date, see you all in the morning," Mr. Elliott says, adding; "Beal, we're all going to sleep a lot better tonight, thanks to your Boston Office."

I get up and begin to put our storyboards back into our portfolio. Tom James comes up to me. He's fuming.

"You're fired!" he says, pointing his finger to within an inch of my nose with a look on his face that reeks of jealousy, envy and complete madness all at the same time.

I can hear Freud. *"There are some neurotics in whom, to judge by all their reactions, the instinct of self-preservation has actually been reversed. They seem to have nothing in view but self-injury and self-destruction. It is possible that people who in the end in fact commit suicide belong to this group."*

"What did he say?" asks Mr. Williams.

"He says he's tired," injects Charlie Boxer, trying to hide the fact that Tom James is a lunatic while at the same time trying to salvage the Regal Hotel account at any cost.

My boss, Joe Haynes, says: "Let's go, Bob, we have some celebrating to do."

"We want Bob Randall, personally, to present his new campaign to Mr. Roberts tomorrow morning," Mr. Elliot says.

This infuriates Tom James even more.

After a round of hand shaking and backslapping, the ITC and Regal clients all depart together and the Boston DDBO contingent heads for the elevators right behind them.

As we get in and the elevator doors close, DDBO chairman, Charlie Boxer, turns to everyone in the elevator and says: "I think we owe a debt of gratitude to Mr. Randall for saving the Regal Hotel account for us tonight."

Tom James just stands in the corner of the elevator with a tortured look of uncontrollable anger twisting his face. If he had a gun he would have shot me on the spot.

Freud said, *"Love cannot be much stronger than the lust to kill. To touch is the beginning of every act of possession, of every attempt to make use of a person or thing."*

The final Tom James flashback

My mind continues to randomly flash through one previous experience to another, suddenly one event that John Austin a copywriter told me about some years ago comes into clear focus.

If it weren't for John, Tom James would be in prison right now, probably for the rest of his life.

John said he was working late one night when he heard two people arguing a dozen partitions away.

"You're going to pay for this."

He said it sounded like Tom James' voice.

"This copy is shit. When I tell you how to write the copy, you don't just do what you want, you do it exactly the way I say to do it."

"That doesn't make any sense, Tom," John heard the other voice defiantly respond. He said it sounded like Chuck Olsen one of the new junior writers.

"I want that copy on my desk before you leave tonight."

"You've got the copy I wrote, in your hand. I'm going home."

John didn't want to get in the middle of an argument between Tom James and one of his subordinate copywriters, that would be occupational suicide.

"You're not going anywhere."

Then John said he suddenly heard the sounds of gurgling and some sort of physical struggle going on.

He waited for a minute and didn't hear any more conversation, just the eerie sound of someone gurgling.

He got up and ran toward the sound.

When he got to the cubicle at the other end of the copy department he discovered Tom James with his knee in Chuck Olsen's chest and his hands around his neck tightly squeezing the life out of him. Chuck's body was folded back over his desk and his face was turning blue, he was limp.

"Get off him, Tom, you'll kill him." John said as he wrapped his arms around Tom James' neck and pulled him off of Chuck Olsen, slamming him against the top of the rippled-glass partition, smashing it to bits.

"Wheeze, wheeze," Chuck restarted his breathing.

"I'll get you for this, Austin." Tom James threatens as he runs down the hall toward his office.

"He's crazy," was all Chuck Olsen could say, gasping for air. "He's crazy."

It's just another one of the many outrageously demented performances of Tom James.

Knowing life at DDBO would never be the same for him, John Austin resigned the next morning.

He's dead as a doornail

How long have I been standing here with my mind flashing through my life? I must be in some kind of state of shock. I once read how survivors of traumatic experiences are, usually unexpectedly, revisited by elements related to the traumatic experience.

I begin to come out of the trance. I suddenly realize I've got to call Detective Breen, right away. He'll know what to do.

I grab the phone on Tom James' desk and dial 9 for an outside line. I rack my brain for Detective Breen's phone number. Maybe I should call him at home…no, I try the precinct first.

I fumble my fingers around the dial. Starting the next number before the rotary dial returns to "ABC."

Stop! Robert, now calm down, take a deep breath and let it out slowly, I tell myself.

After a few deep breaths, I begin to dial more calmly.

"13th Precinct," comes out of the phone.

"I'm Robert Randall, I'm looking for Detective Frank Breen."

"He doesn't work here anymore, he retired last year."

"Thanks, I'll try him at home."

"Okay, he should be there, do you have his home number?"

"No, I'm not sure what it is."

"It's Davenport 6-7642."

I grab a pencil from the chrome cylinder on Tom's desk and scribble it on a piece of his personalized notepaper.

"Thanks."

I click down the disconnect button on the cradle, and dial Detective Breen's home number.

"Hello?" I recognize the voice, it's Frank's wife, Edna.

"Mrs. Breen, this is Robert Randall, is Detective Breen there?"

"Why hello Robert, it's been a long time since we've heard from you. How are you?"

"I'm fine Mrs. Breen. Can I talk to Detective Breen?

"He's retired now, he's not a detective any more."

"That's all right, I need to talk to him. It's very important."

"Oh, why yes, of course, Robert. Frank it's for you."

"Hello, Frank Breen."

"Detective Breen, this it Robert Randall."

"How are you Robert, it's been a long time. How's the job in Boston going for you?"

"It's fine, but I'm not in Boston right now and I'm in a lot of trouble."

"What kind of trouble?"

It's at this instant that I realize that Tom James' body is on the floor on the other side of the desk.

"Errrr...I'm standing over the body of the agency's top creative boss. I'm in his office here in New York City. It looks like he has been murdered."

"Why do you think that?"

"The window looks like it has been shattered from the outside and there's glass all over the floor. I think he may have been shot from the hotel across the street, there's blood on the floor."

As I look down at Tom's body, it dawns on me that the blood pattern next to him looks like a blazing red Rorschach test that seems to be trying to tell me something.

"Is he breathing?"

"I don't know."

"Did you check his pulse?"

"I'm too scared to."

"Calm down now, Robert, put down the phone and go over and put your finger on the carotid artery in his neck, under his chin, and see if you feel any pulse."

"All right."

I put the phone on the desk and go over to Tom James. His eyes are open and staring at the ceiling. He looks like he's alive. I hold my hand in front of his eyes so I don't have to see him looking at me. I reach under his chin and feel for a pulse in his neck. He is cold and there doesn't appear to be any pulse.

I go back and pick up the phone. "I don't feel any pulse, he's cold, I think he's dead."

"Okay, Robert, now listen to me. Don't touch anything else in the room."

"Okay."

"Where is this office located?"

"It's on Madison Avenue, between 46th and 47th Street. The number is 385. Use the right bank of elevators."

"What floor?"

"Twelfth. His office is in the back right-hand corner of the building, overlooking Vanderbilt Avenue and Grand Central Station."

"What's the man's name?"

"He's Tom James, the worldwide creative director of the agency."

"I'll make the call to the 18th Precinct to report the murder, they should be there in about 20-minutes. In the meantime Robert, don't let anybody into that office. I'll get there as soon as I can."

"Okay, thanks, but the office is deserted, everyone has gone home."

"Just be sure nobody touches anything until the police arrive."

"Okay."

I begin to feel a bit calmer, just knowing Detective Breen is on his way here?

It's a little creepy with Tom James' body on the floor, so I decide to cover it. I take one of the side chairs, slide it over to the window and take down one of the drapes and put it over Tom James. It makes me feel better.

I find a spot to relax on the floor in the corner next to one of the wingback chairs opposite Tom's desk, as far away from his body as I can get.

I touch the tips of my fingers together, cross my legs, and take a deep breath letting it out very slowly, while releasing the traditional meditation sound. "Ohmmmmmmm."

In a minute I'm feeling better. I'm glad my old swimming coach, Ed Cashin, taught us this meditation technique of the Tibetan monks, to calm us down before our swim meets.

But no matter how much I try to calm down and meditate, I just can't seem to do it completely. My mind is still crammed with a hodgepodge of images spanning the last 10-years. Who could have killed Tom James?

"Ohmmmmmmm," I continue my meditation.

The police arrive

In the distance, I hear the sounds of at least two police officers coming down the hall toward Tom James' office. A fully equipped police officer makes a distinct sound as he walks, all the equipment; gun, cuffs, nightstick, and whistle jingle in tempo with his gait, even the leather belt and holster squeak in the same rhythm.

"Ching, creek, ching, creek."

"That's the office down there in the corner where the light's on." I hear the voice of Phil, the night watchman, telling the cops.

"Thanks, we'll take it from here."

As the one of the officers appears in the doorway, the first thing I notice is the silver precinct numbers on the tips of his collars, "18th Precinct."

"Are you Robert Randall?" he asks.

"Yes, I am."

"Frank Breen told us you were here."

The second officer rushes over to Tom James pulls back the drape and puts his fingers on his neck to confirm he's dead.

"No pulse."

The first policeman looks at me a little puzzled, "What are you doing sitting there on the floor?"

"I've been meditating to calm myself down."

"I'm patrolman Clancy O'Brien and he's Pete Gordon." "Are you all right? You do look a little dazed."

"I guess I've been in a kind of trance. My brain has been streaming endless images of almost everything I have experienced here at DDBO over the past 10-years.

"Who is this guy?" He points his thumb in the direction of Tom James' body as he takes a small notebook from his shirt pocket flips over the pages and begins to write.

"Pete, what's today's date?"

"The 23rd. Want the year?"

"I know the year."

"He's Tom James, the worldwide creative director of this agency."

"DDBO?"

"Yes, that's right."

"I saw the name on the directory in the lobby."

I get up and go and sit in one of the side chairs.

"What happened?"

"When I saw Tom James dead, I guess my life started to flash before me."

"No, I mean how did he get killed?"

"I don't know. When I got to my hotel room tonight after the Regal Hotel meeting, earlier in the day, here at the agency, there was a message from him demanding that I come and see him in his office immediately. When I got here this is how I found him."

"What time did you arrive?"

"It was around eleven."

"Did you see anybody?"

"Only the night watchman, Phil, and the elevator operator on duty in the lobby."

"Was there anyone else up here?"

"No, no one was around, everyone had gone home. The cleaners had put out most of the lights."

"Do you have any idea what happened?"

"Not really."

"Who broke the window?"

"The only thing I can think of is that it looks like someone may have shot him from the Roosevelt Hotel across the street. That's why all the glass is inside the room, it broke inward from the impact of a bullet or something."

"Pretty smart deduction."

"Elementary, Officer O'Brien." I couldn't help but paraphrase Sherlock Holmes' most famous line, actually Sir Arthur Conan Doyle's most famous line.

The patrolman smiles as he pulls out his handkerchief and picks up the phone.

"I used that phone earlier to call Detective Breen, so my prints will be on it."

The detective nods his head, "Yes, Detective Breen of the 13th Precinct, how do you know him?"

I met him 10-years ago, I helped him solve my great uncle's murder."

"You did, isn't he retired?"

"Yes, but he's on his way here right now."

"Oh, good, retired or not, he's a good detective."

The patrolman proceeds to dial.

"Bill? This is Clancy we need the full homicide crime scene investigation team over here right away…one body…a man…some big shot at this advertising agency…looks like he's been shot…we'll want ballistics on the bullet…oh, we're at 385 Madison Avenue, 12th floor… I'll have Pete Gordon meet them down at the elevator in the lobby."

Thank God, Detective Breen arrives

"Robert, how are you, young man? I got here as fast as I could."

It is so good to see Detective Breen, looking and sounding more like Humphrey Bogart than ever.

"Hello, Detective Breen, I'm officer Clancy O'Brien and this is Pete Gordon, we're from the 18th Precinct."

"I think we've met before at one of the Department Communion Breakfasts."

I can start to feel my heart rate slow down and my whole body starts to relax, "Am I glad to see you, Detective Breen."

I never realized that meeting Detective Frank Breen back in 1954 would play such an important role in my life today. I was going to art school at the Flatiron Building at the time and trying to find my great uncle William's killer.

"What happened here, Robert?"

I point to Tom James on the floor, "That man is Tom James, the Worldwide Creative Director of DDBO."

"You said on the phone."

"I last saw him alive earlier this evening at the emergency Regal Hotel meeting in the agency's boardroom on the 11th floor."

"Emergency meeting?"

"Yes, the meeting was with one of the agency's largest accounts,

Regal Hotels, the CEO of Regal's parent company had killed the current advertising campaign and taken it off the air. It is costing the agency a bundle in missed commissions. And when they find out what happened in the meeting, they're going to think I did it."

"Why?"

"Because Tom James and I had a major confrontation regarding the campaign that should replace the one that was pulled."

"What happened?"

"He wanted them to buy his idea, but they weren't going for it. My boss from the Boston office of DDBO, Joe Haynes, insisted that I present the approach that the Regal Hotels client, Morton Williams, had asked us to develop in Boston, and when the client liked it Tom James went berserk."

"What did he do?"

"He fired me on the spot."

"Wow, in the meeting?"

"Yes." And when I got back to my room at the Park Regal Hotel tonight there was a message from him to come here immediately. When I got here this is how I found him. And then I called you."

"You did the right thing, Robert."

Suddenly, we all feel a hot breeze wafting in through the broken window.

"You think someone killed him from the hotel across the street?"

"As I told the policemen, the glass appears to have broken inward, possibly indicating that something pierced it from the outside, and it looks like Tom was shot."

"Good thinking Robert, I can see you haven't lost your detective skills."

"Clancy, is it okay if we go next door to the hotel?"

"Frank, why don't you wait until the homicide detectives get here, then you can ask them. They're going to be in charge of this case. I'm sure they won't have a problem with your going over there."

"Right, that's what we'll do."

Just then as Detective Been finishes his response, we hear voices outside approaching the office.

"Clancy, how you doing?"

"Good, Al, how are you?"

The detectives arrive.

"This is Detective Breen from the 13th and this is Robert Randall, he works here."

"Actually, I work in the Boston office."

"Robert tells me the stiff is Tom James, this is his office, it looks like he was shot from the hotel over there."

"Detective Breen, didn't you put in your papers, last year?"

"That's right Al, Robert here, called me when he found the body. He and I had worked on his great uncle's murder case back in 1954, and he called me and asked me to come down to help him."

"Robert, I'm Detective Al Ward of the 18th Precinct."

"Good to meet you."

"So you helped Frank solve your great uncle's murder? I'm impressed."

"Yes, I did."

"Frank, how would you like to help us with this case?"

"I'd be glad to, it'll get me out of the house."

"And you'll earn that pension."

"Robert, is it possible for you to work with Frank on this case?"

"I think so, I'll ask my boss if I can take a couple of days off."

"Good, let me know, we can use all the help we can get. We're up to our eyeballs in homicides, and you know a lot about this guy and this company."

"Frank, what are your first instincts on this murder?"

"As Robert suggested, it looks like the bullet came in the window from the hotel across the street. I think it might be a good idea if Robert and I go over there to see if we can take a look in those rooms right across the way. Maybe we can find who might have been in them tonight. We'll be careful not to disturb any forensic evidence we find. We'll call you to let you know which room to send the crime scene team to."

"Good, we'll stay here until the Medical Examiner arrives, to see if we can dig up any clues. Check in with us, later."

"Okay, we'll give you a call in a little while."

Detective Breen and I go to the Roosevelt Hotel

It is still a very hot night as we exit through the revolving door of 385 Madison Avenue turn left and go to the corner. We walk over the subway grates in the sidewalk and are treated with a refreshing blast of cool air from the trains traveling in the tunnel beneath us. We continue across 46th Street into the side revolving door of the Roosevelt Hotel, marching up the staircase to the lobby and across the tattered paisley pattern carpet, following the highlighted path of wear to the front desk.

"I'm Detective Frank Breen," Frank announces, holding up his old badge for the clerk to see." He obviously had a feeling he'd be working on the case and he brought his badge and his gun with him.

"What can I do for you, Detective Breen?"

"We want to take a look at a couple of rooms up on the twelfth floor in the back corner of the hotel at Vanderbilt and 46th Street."

"Why, may I ask?"

"We believe someone may have fired a gun from one of those rooms at the building across the street."

"Fired a gun?"

"That's right, do you know the numbers of those rooms?"

"Why yes, of course."

"Can you tell me who was in those rooms, tonight?"

"Let me look it up for you."

"That would be rooms 1211, 1212 and 1213 at the corner. Rooms 1211 and 1212 weren't occupied tonight. Room 1213 is occupied at the moment."

"Who is it registered to?"

"A Mister John Smith."

"Oh, one of those, don't you guys ever ask for identification?"

"I wasn't the one who checked him in, Detective."

"Can you have someone accompany us up to the room with a key?"

"I can give you the key."

"No, I want a hotel employee to go with us."

"Very well, wait a minute."

Within a few minutes, the Bell Captain arrives and we proceed to the elevator. Soon we are exiting from the elevator on the 12th floor. The hall is dark and dingy, and as in the lobby, the carpet shows endless footsteps of wear down the center. We follow the Bell Captain to the end of the hall.

We want the corner room, 1213.

"Here it is, sir."

"Okay, open it up and the both of you stand aside," Detective Breen orders, as he draws his gun from it's holster under his left shoulder. A definite sign that he thought this was going to be a serious case.

The Bell Captain turns the key in the lock, pushes the door open and jumps back. Detective Breen slowly enters the room.

"Anybody here?"

There's no answer.

"Wait until I check the room out."

In less than a minute he announces, "All clear."

We move into the room.

"Don't touch anything."

Detective Breen freezes in his tracks.

"Do you smell that?"

"What is it?"

"It definitely smells like a gun has recently been fired in this room."

It's then that my nostrils sense the sharp pungent odor of sulfur permeating the air. Like when I did an experiment with my "Gilbert Chemistry Set" when I was a kid.

"Whoever was in this room is long gone."

"Frank, it looks like the murderer fired the gun out this window and then closed it."

"I think you're right, Robert."

"Look Frank, we can see Detective Ward very clearly over in Tom James' office."

"Robert, do you have the number to Tom James' office?"

"Yes, I think I do," I start searching through my jacket pockets for the hotel note paper where I had written the number, that I had gotten from the hotel operator earlier tonight, for the direct line to Tom James' office.

"I want to call Detective Ward to let him know what we have found."

"Here's the number."

"Good, can you let us in the room next door so we can use the phone?"

"Yes sir."

We march out to the next room and the Bell Captain opens the door.

"Now you go back to 1213 and guard the door until the police crime scene investigation team arrives. Don't let anybody in the room, no one."

"Yes, sir."

Breen picks up the phone and dials, "Detective Ward? This is Detective Breen. There definitely was a gun fired in this room tonight, the odor is so sharp you can cut it with a knife. Judging by the strength of the smell it probably was a rifle that was fired. No, we didn't touch a thing. Better get the crime scene team over here as soon as possible. Of course, the room was registered to a John Smith. Yeah, I told them the same thing. Right, I have the Bell Captain guarding the door until your men get here. Robert and I will check in with you tomorrow. Good-bye."

"Detective Breen, I think we should go see Tom James' wife, Hilda, tomorrow."

"Good idea, where does she live?"

"Up in Scarsdale, New York?"

"Do you know how to get there?"

"Yes, meet me in Grand Central, under the clock at 10 a.m. and we'll go pay her a visit."

"I'll be there, see you in the morning, Robert."

"Goodnight."

We leave the hotel and head back out into the hot night air. I'm still wondering who the murderer could be as I head back to my hotel.

It's no surprise Tom James is murdered

When I get back to my room at the Park Regal Hotel, it's after midnight and there's another message for me. I'm almost too afraid to find out who it's from. It turns out, the message is from Carl MacDougall the account supervisor on the Regal Hotel account; he wants me to join them in his room for a party, no matter how late it is.

I call his room, "Carl, are you guys still partying?"

"You bet your life, Randall, get your ass up here."

When I get to the room I find the door open and Carl leading the celebration with the whole Boston contingent. He's waving a bottle of champagne in one hand and a glass in the other, pushing them both toward me.

"Hi, Bob, come on in and join the celebration. It's you we're celebrating. You did a great job tonight. You really stuck it to Tom James."

"He's dead."

"Who's dead?" asks Joe Haynes, the manager of the Boston office, with a look of both total disbelief and joy on his prematurely wrinkled face at the same time. He spends a lot of time down at the Cape fishing and the sun has accented all the wrinkles around his eyes. When he squints while fishing the creases in his skin don't get any sun so when he's in the office and not squinting the creases are white, a very strange effect.

"Tom James, he was murdered tonight in his office!" "How do you know that?"

The sounds of shock fill the room.

"I just came from there. He left me a message, demanding that I go to his office tonight. I found him dead when I got there."

"You did? Who murdered him?"

"I don't know the police are working on that now."

"Well, it's not going to be easy, there must be a couple of hundred people who would like to see him dead," Carl says, as he takes a big gulp of champagne.

"I'm sure I'll be at the top of their list, after today's meeting."

"You saved the Regal Hotel account."

"Joe, would it be all right if I take the next couple of days off?"

"Sure. Why?"

"I want to stay down here to work with the police to see if I can help them find out who killed Tom."

"You do? Work with the police?"

"Yes, back in 1954, I worked with a New York police detective named Frank Breen, to solve my great uncle William's murder."

"You did? Your great uncle William's murder?"

"It's a long story, I'll tell you all about it when I get back to Boston in a few days."

"Okay, Robert, but don't forget you have a command performance before "Killer Roberts" tomorrow morning. "Oh, that's right. I'll have to let Detective Breen know."

"Then call me tomorrow afternoon, in Boston, to see if we need to ask you anything about the jobs that are in the works up there."

"Win Miller knows everything about every job we're working on, Joe, and I am available by phone to answer any questions and make any decisions, if necessary."

"All right Robert, you be careful. This is a really weird situation."

"Detective Breen is a smart old bird, he'll take care of me. I'll let you know what happens. We're going up to see Tom's wife tomorrow."

"Has somebody told her about his death?"

"I'm not sure. Goodnight, guys, keep the party going."

"Will do, Bob, goodnight."

"Joe, I'll see you back in Boston in a couple of days."

"Take care, Bob, if you need any help, let us know," Charlie Jones adds.

"I'm heading back to my room to try to get some sleep, thanks."

As I get out into the hallway, I start thinking about the one person who might be able to shed some light on Tom James' murder, my old boss in New York, Sven Svenson, he's been at the agency for a long time and if anyone knows where the skeletons are hidden it's him. I'll go to see him in the morning after the ITC meeting and before Detective Breen and I go to see Tom's wife. But right now, I better let Detective Breen know I'll be late.

Goodbye, loser

It's the next morning and I'm in the ITC boardroom overlooking Park Avenue, surrounded again by the entire ITC, Regal Hotel, and DDBO teams. Thanks to our new campaign the tone is much more friendly and jovial.

Mr. Elliott stands up at the head of the table, "Mr. Roberts returned from Europe late last night. He's anxious to see the new campaign you did, Bob. I want to thank you for coming up with the new idea."

"You're welcome."

"Why don't you sit at the head of the table, it'll make it easier for you to make the presentation."

I reposition myself.

In strolls William Earnest, the son of the late founder of Regal Hotels. He was the largest stockholder before the unfriendly buyout, but now ITC is the largest stockholder, which, I don't think he fully grasps the impact of. It's clear he has none of his father's entrepreneurial talent; he's just a spoiled rich kid who rode through life on his father's coat tails. He's grossly overweight with a thin pencil moustache, a rather comical combination, looking more like Oliver Hardy then Errol Flynn. He has his overcoat draped on his shoulders over his jacket and his gray suede gloves held tightly in his right hand snapping them into his left palm like he's some kind of royalty. God knows why, he apparently has decided to oppose Mr. Roberts' demand to change the campaign. Possibly he believes he had something to do with its creation, which is definitely not the case. He moves directly to the head of the table.

"You sit over there," he points for me to move.

I do so.

Suddenly the entire ITC team stands up and snaps to military attention.

Mr. Roberts comes marching through the door, stops at the head of the table and motions for Mr. Earnest to move. Mr. Earnest is stunned, his face turns red and he reluctantly gets up and demands my seat, again.

I quickly relinquish it to him and move to the end of the table.

"Where's the new campaign I asked for?" Mr. Roberts bellows.

"Before we look at the new campaign, I want to say something."

Everyone's attention is instantly directed at Mr. Earnest with expressions of disbelief covering their faces. Some of them actually pulling their heads back in total shock. They obviously know what happens to a person who challenges the great "Killer Roberts."

"Oh?" is all that Mr. Roberts says, obviously somewhat surprised at Mr. Earnest's impertinence.

We all watch Mr. Earnest as he proceeds to lose his job through a series of ridiculously stupid incoherent ramblings on totally unrelated subjects. Starting with a cockamamie story about polishing shoes in the army, with a ridiculous reference to a spit and polished hotel, which makes absolutely no sense to anyone. Followed by an outrageously detailed description of the proper way to make a hotel bed. At no time during the next twenty minutes does he ever mention his objection to killing the present Regal Hotels advertising campaign, the supposed reason he demanded to be included in this meeting. After 30-minutes Mr. Earnest finally stops ranting.

The room becomes so silent that a proverbial pin dropping would deafen us all.

All eyes in the room pivot to Mr. Roberts, who says, with absolutely no expression on his face, "You're excused from this meeting, Mr. Earnest."

Mr. Earnest gets up and exits the room staring into space.

"Now, where is my new campaign, boys?"

"Bob Randall here, from DDBO, has the new campaign." Mr. Elliott announces.

"All right, Bob, show us what you've got.

I proceed to present the campaign that I presented in the DDBO boardroom the night before.

"That's it, good job Bob, run with it." Mr. Roberts stands and unceremoniously exits the boardroom.

Mr. Elliott quickly runs to the door and closes it.

The entire group in the meeting jumps to their feet and give me a round of applause.

I suddenly realize that in this insane business of advertising, there will be times when I will benefit from its insanity. Now I head to Sven's office.

Sven spills a few secrets of his own

"Sven?"

"Yes, Robert, come in. How are things going up in Boston?"

"Great."

"What can I do for you?" He gets up from the layout he is working on at his desk and takes off his glasses, looking quite serious. He's a classy guy. He has an elegant French provincial desk with a custom drawing board mounted in the center.

"Have you heard about Tom James' death, Robert?"

"Yes, I was the one who found him."

"How did that happen?"

"He and I had a confrontation in yesterday's Regal Hotel meeting and he demanded that I come and see him last night."

"Well, to be honest I don't think anyone is surprised."

"Joe Haynes is letting me take the next couple of days off to help with the case."

"Oh?"

"Frank Breen, a retired police detective who has volunteered to assist the 18th Precinct with Tom's murder investigation has asked me to work with him."

"Really?"

"Well, I worked with him on my great uncle's murder 10-years ago."

"Your great uncle's murder?"

"That's right, my great uncle was murdered at the Flatiron Building in 1922. I ended up going to art school there and because he was my great uncle and had access to a lot of private family information, Detective Breen thought it would be smart if I worked with him on the case. As it turned out, it was beneficial to solving the mystery."

"That's interesting."

"Detective Breen thinks that my experience of having worked with Tom could help him understand the way the advertising business works and give him some insights into Tom's personality and lifestyle."

"That's right, you did work with Tom on the Norman Cosmetics account. But I will never forget that meeting with Sandy Burnstein."

"I came here to see if you can tell me anything unusual that has happened to Tom over the past several years, since I transferred up to Boston."

Sven ponders for a moment, putting the earpiece of his glasses into his mouth and raising his eyebrows. "Well, there have been a number of weird incidents that have involved Tom James."

"Can you tell me about them?"

"There's no question Tom had a very strong, pejorative personality. Not too many people liked him."

"What about the incidents?"

"First, there was the time he became emotional unstable and completely unglued at a meeting in his office, last year. He had called a group to his office to resolve the crisis on the General Brands account. The client had demanded that the agency find a way to fight the government's plan to legislate a new tax on the liquor industry. Tom seemed not to be able to handle the assignment. Every time someone would make a suggestion he would start screaming and putting the person down with his usual crude brand of ruthless, personal character assassinations. He kept saying that management wouldn't buy any of their ideas. It was as if he had some inside knowledge about the company. It was brutal. Within less than 15-minutes, everyone had had enough of his paranoid antics and they all stormed out of the meeting en masse. Tom put his head down on his desk and began to bawl like a baby. He was pathetic."

"Who was in that meeting?"

"Let me see, there was Gary Miller an account executive, Phyllis Plunkett a copywriter, Larry Almgren an art director, Bill Palmer another copywriter and Helen Collyer from the Public Relations Department."

I quickly jot down the names of the DDBO people who were there. I have been carrying a small notebook ever since I worked with detective Breen 10-years ago.

"Are there any other incidents that you can think of?"

"There was the time Tom was accused of being bi-sexual."

"Who did that?"

"It wasn't a who, it was anonymous, someone had snuck into the mail room at night and put a number of envelopes in the boxes of the Board of Directors. The envelopes contained the details of a relationship that Tom James was supposedly having with a new young male copywriter. They reportedly spent a lot of time together. The letter sighted the times they had checked into a local hotel and stayed in the same room. And a time when they went to a client convention and shared the same room.

Only the Board of Directors got copies of the letter. I got a copy. I always thought Tom was just mentoring the young man, nothing was ever proven, although a few of the directors did ask for his resignation."

"Who were the directors who wanted him to resign?"

"I believe there were three of them. Ronald Carpenter, 2-E Jones and John Newton."

"How is Jones' first name spelled?"

"With the number "2" and the letter "E." His real name is Edward Everett Jones, so he calls himself 2-E, but most people think his name is Touey. Would you believe his mother named him after the movie star, Edward Everett Horton, because she was infatuated with him, 2-E never forgave her."

"Are they all still with the agency?"

"Yes."

"Can you think of any other strange incidents involving Tom James?"

"Only one, Tom had an argument with one of the clients at last year's General Brands convention held at the Montauk Point hotel.

"Those people are crazy, I went to one of those conventions, a couple of years ago, when I was working here in New York."

"Well apparently Tom had gone out there to pitch a new campaign to them, and during the presentation, the president of General Brands, abruptly stopped Tom and started to berate him about the agency not doing anything about the liquor tax Washington was about to pass. Tom exploded and started yelling at him calling him a gangster and threatening to have him investigated. It was another one of Tom's psychiatric moments, the next morning Tom had left before breakfast."

"Who is the president of General Brands?"

"He's a tough guy named Salvatore Vanucci, the rumor is that he was a bootlegger in the 20's during prohibition and that's how he started General Brands."

"In art school those of us who were preparing to go into the advertising business were required to study psychology. One of the classes was about psychoses. A psychosis is a break with reality. The ultimate psychosis is schizophrenia. The most common symptoms are incoherent thinking, lack of emotional response, delusions and hallucinations. Schizophrenics are prone to interpret certain words to mean totally different things. They become paranoiac with delusions of persecution leading them not to trust anyone – not even their own family."

"That's very interesting, Robert."

Suddenly the image of Tom's enraged face with his eyes bulging pops into my head. I can hear him yelling, "Randall, you're either with me or against me."

I switch my attention back to Sven. "Sven, thanks for all your help, if you think of anything else please let me know."

"Alright Robert, you be careful now."

We pay a visit to Tom's wife, Hilda

I take the back elevator down to the ground floor rear lobby, go past Cherry's Lounge and out onto Vanderbilt Avenue. I walk two blocks south to one of the secret doors that I know of that leads down to the vast underground labyrinth of passages, staircases and corridors ending up in Grand Central Station. As I descend the dimly lit staircase I think about some of the fascinating tidbits I have learned about this subterranean man-made cavern. Apparently there's a mysterious "Track 61," 30-feet below the famous 40-story Waldorf Astoria on Park Avenue. It has been a favorite destination of "urban explorers" since the 1940's. Reportedly there's a bulletproof freight car, sitting in the dark, on this track 61 that was used by President Franklin Delano Roosevelt to gain concealed access to downtown New York City. The Secret Service would drive his armor-plated Pierce Arrow off of the train onto the track 61 platform and into an awaiting elevator that would then take him up into the hotel garage. President Roosevelt could take his private train back and forth between Hyde Park and Grand Central Station without anyone ever knowing. Track 61 amounted to a private railway siding for the Waldorf Astoria and many wealthy guests of the time would have their private rail cars routed directly to the hotel siding and take a private passenger elevator up to their suites. During World War II this massive cavern housed the special rotary current converters that changed AC current to DC to run the trains along the entire Eastern Seaboard. It's said that Adolf Hitler dispensed two spies to sabotage the facility. The spies were arrested before they could strike. A stairway runs from the platform on track 61 up to hidden street entrances on 49th and 50th Streets. The odor down here is a combination of the cold steel, ozone from the electric trains and oily smoke from the diesel engines. Finally I go through a long dimly lit tunnel and out into a side foyer of Grand Central Station. The noise level rises dramatically. Every time I come here I think of the 1940's radio program of the same name.

"Grand Central Station, crossroads of a million private lives! A gigantic stage on which are played a thousand dramas daily!" was the last lines of the opening narrative. Every day a different story would start in the station and end somewhere else in the city.

I go directly to the large clock at the circular information counter in the center of the gigantic main terminal area. Hundreds of people are hustling and bustling everywhere.

It's about 10-minutes to 10. I spot the familiar figure leaning against the counter.

"Good morning, Detective Breen."

"Morning Robert, you're right on time. Where do we go from here?"

"Over there to that ticket counter on the far side."

We get round-trip tickets to White Plains, and then head down to the platform for the train to Scarsdale.

I think back to the first time I met Hilda at the agency's vice-president's party, last year, when I was made a vice president. I was the youngest vice-president to be named in the history of the agency, up to that point. Something that Tom James hated me for, because he was two years older when he made vice-president. He mentioned it every time we met, "Just because you made vice president at 29, Randall, doesn't mean shit to me, you never went to college, you only went to some stupid art school."

At this time of the morning there's not many trains heading up to the north, they're still all coming down into the city. We walk down the ramp to the Scarsdale train. To be sure, I go into the first car looking for the conductor. I spot him. "Does this train stop at Scarsdale?"

"Yes, it does, in 1-hour and 45-minutes from now."

"Okay, thanks. When does it leave?"

"In 30-minutes."

"Thanks."

"Well, Detective Breen, we're going to have some waiting to do."

"That's no problem, why don't we go back to the terminal for a cup of coffee?"

"Sounds good to me."

On the way to the coffee shop I can't help but remember a senior art director named Suren Almasian, an Armenian guy who traveled to the city from Westport, Connecticut every day.

I tell Frank the story, "Every Friday on the way home while most commuters crowded into the bar car to get sloshed, Suren was part of a group of ad guys who took over the platform between the last two cars to shoot craps. Just before 5-o'clock he would run down to the bank to cash his check, stuff a huge wad of bills into his jacket pocket and race to the train. And almost every Friday he would lose it all, every dollar, before he got to the Westport station. Everyone wondered how he could pay his bills, until it was discovered that his wife was the president of her own agency – Joan Wells Advertising – lucky for him she made a lot more money than he did, and she didn't gamble."

"He sounds like quite a character."

"He's very talented."

After a mediocre cup of coffee in the Terminal Coffee Shop and a mesmerizingly boring ride to Scarsdale followed by a brief taxi ride we are standing at the front door to Hilda James' home. Detective Breen pushes the bell. We wait for about a minute but no one answers the door. Detective Breen pushes the bell again.

"Maybe she's not home."

"Hold on, Robert, be patient, we've come a long way."

After another few minutes the door opens.

"Can I help you?" A beautifully made-up Hilda James asks, appearing as if she hasn't spent a single moment grieving over her dead husband.

"I'm Detective Breen and this is Robert Randall, we're here to ask you a few questions about your husband's death."

She recognizes me right away.

"I'm sorry about Tom's death, Hilda."

"Robert, what are you doing here?"

"I'm working with Detective Breen on Tom's murder."

"You are?"

"Mrs. James, can we come in?"

"Why, yes, of course, please come in."

Hilda looks just as I remember her, a petite, slim, woman with beauty shop jet-black hair and impeccable makeup. She's in the latest fashions from Fifth Avenue. A short, dark blue Coco Chanel dress designed with a pattern of soft blue flowers, accented with splashes of red poppies, clings to her athletically trim body like a one-piece nylon bathing suit. As she enters her living room in front of us, I glance down to see that the calves of her legs are sculpted like those of an Olympic runner. The flimsy fabric of her dress accents her muscular thighs narrowing at the knees. My eyes continue to scan down to see two perfect and delicately thin ankles.

"Please sit down," she gestures, pointing to two large chairs in the living room.

"We're very sorry about your husband, Mrs. James."

"Thank you. Have you found out who killed him?"

"Not yet, that's what we're trying to find out."

"Do you know of any reason why anyone would want to kill your husband?"

"Well, as I'm sure Robert has told you, he was a very troubled person and did have many enemies in the advertising business."

"What do you mean?"

"He had an unusual upbringing, his parents were radio performers who had their own radio show. They were quite famous and always in the spotlight, Tom found it difficult to deal with it. It made him very insecure. He had been going to counselors ever since he was a child."

"Shrinks?"

"Yes, child psychiatrists. I think they only made his problems worse. He didn't know he had any problems until they began to name them and give him detailed descriptions of them. Which, I think, caused him to act them out."

"Hilda, has he ever been violent to you or any of the children?"

Her face freezes.

I must have hit a vital cord.

"Would you like something to drink, Robert?" was her disconnected response as she jumps up and almost runs out of the room.

"Robert, I think you hit a nerve."

"I only heard of Tom being violent twice, once in the office, when he tried to strangle a copywriter, and once at the company outing where he took a swing at another copywriter during a softball game at the "Westchester Country Club."

Hilda returns, "Here you are," she hands us each a glass of what looks and tastes like iced tea.

"Thank you."

"Mrs. James, did your husband ever hit you or any of the children?" Breen asks again.

"There was a few times he lost his temper and spanked the boys."

"Did he ever hit you?"

"Only once, when I asked him if he was having an affair with one of the associate creative directors. It incensed him and he just exploded."

"Did he hurt you?"

"He swung at me and I pulled away and he only grazed my face," she coolly responds.

"Was that the only time?"

"Yes, he said he was very sorry and never did it again."

"Who was the associate creative director you suspected him of having an affair with?"

"Marilyn Kennedy."

"He was such a aggressively rude person in the office, it's hard to believe he was different at home, Mrs. James."

"There were times when his malevolent actions were a kind of violence all their own."

Hilda sensually crosses her legs, trying to take our attention off our line of questioning, but frank continues.

"Did you ever have to step in when he had a fight with one of the children?"

"No, I was afraid to."

"Did you ever have to call the police because of his violent actions?"

"No."

"Well, thank you Mrs. James, we'll get back to you if we have any further questions."

"Thank you Detective Breen. Robert, it is good to see you again."

"Thank you, Hilda. Sorry about Tom."

Although I felt sorry for Hilda and her children, I actually wasn't all that sad that Tom was dead.

She did it, or did she?

On the way back to New York City I tell Frank one of my theories, "One of he first persons I thought could have killed Tom James is his wife Hilda. She could have murdered him or had somebody do it for her. She is one very cool lady. It doesn't take much imagination to realize that if dozens of people who work with him had a motive to kill him, who would have a better motive than the person he could have been abusing every day and night, his wife. She could have done it to protect her four children, who he could have been brutally abusing."

"Robert, it looks like we're going to have to talk to some of the neighbors, and check with the local police, to see what we can find out."

"Something tells me, that when we get back to the City, tonight, I should go over to Tom James' office to check some things out."

"His office will probably be locked."

"Can I get the key at the 18th Precinct?"

"I'll give them a call to make sure they have completed their crime scene investigation. Stop by there to get a key."

"Good, thanks. I'm not sure why, but something is telling me to go back there."

Cutting "Gordian's knot"

It's late, when I finally get to the lobby of the DDBO New York office.

The night watchman greets me. "Hello, Robert, what are you doing here, tonight?"

"Hi, Phil, I have permission from the police to check out Tom James' office, they gave me the key."

"Okay, go ahead."

As I get to the 12th floor and start the long, dark familiar walk back to Tom James' office, a haunting feeling comes over me. It's as if it's a late night and I'm coming from my old office, after working on some tune-in ads for Global Broadcasting. Tonight, as usual, everyone has gone home. The cleaning crew has finished their job and turned out the lights leaving the copy department totally dark. It's not unusual, it happened every time I worked late. But tonight it's very eerie. As I walk, I contemplate the darkness, thinking about the mystery of Tom James' murder. It is so complex I feel like Alexander the Great must have felt when he was presented with Gordian's knot. As the story goes, the Phrygian's were without a king. The priests had declared that the next man to enter the city of Gordium driving a cart would become king. Midas, a poor peasant was that man. Midas didn't want the job, so, he dedicates his father's ox cart to the god Sabazios, supposedly tying the ox to a post at the entrance to the city with an intricate knot of cornel bark, announcing: "The one who would untie the knot would become king of Asia Minor."

Alexander arrived and attempted to untie the knot. Having found no end to the knot he simply split it in two with a mighty blow of his sword, thereby becoming king.

I think that's what we need here, a powerful force to solve Tom James' killing.

I continue to feel my way through the copy department, stopping occasionally and looking back to the rays of light coming from the elevator lobby to get my bearings. Now I'm guided by the glow coming in the windows of the offices along 46th Street.

"Ralph, are you here?" I call out to the empty copy department, not wanting to be surprised again by the agency's resident "Peeping Tom."

I thankfully get no reply, so I continue to Tom James' office. The door is still closed; they have not reassigned the office to anyone yet, although there are many vultures circling to land there. When somebody leaves the copy department the empty office is usually filled the next day, there's a written "pecking order" in Tom's secretary's deck.

I don't really know what is driving me to be here, I just feel a strange force compelling me. The key that I picked up at the 18th Precinct unlocks the door, I turn the knob and the door swings open. My heart feels a burst of mysterious energy, I'm afraid, I have no idea what I'm going to find. I haven't been here since Tom's death, the other night. Then, as the door fully swings open, I see it. A jade-green form just like the one I saw back in the art school storage room, when I was working on solving my Great Uncle Williams murder. It begins to take shape.

"Great Uncle William, is that you?"

The mystical protoplasmic form slowly continues to take the shape of a transparent human.

I feel the same nervous sensation sweeping over my body that I felt back in art school.

The surge in my chest grows to enormous proportions.

I can't believe what I am seeing. It's Tom James.

"Tom, is that you?"

The eerie form doesn't answer, but motions for me to remove the painting from the wall behind the desk.

I feel myself automatically driven to follow its direction.

The painting is heavy and the wire is hanging on two hooks on the wall.

The form gestures me to put it face down on the desk.

At this moment, my peripheral vision senses the bright green reflection of the blob undulating in the office windows. It must really be here if I can see it reflected in the windows.

There is a sliver of a cut barely visible in the paper backing at the corner of the painting.

If the green form hadn't pointed it out to me, I probably would never have found it. Its no wonder the crime scene team didn't see it.

I peel open the slit. There is a white envelope that has been hidden inside behind the brown paper. I slide it out and put it on the desk. The form motions for me to put the painting back.

I lift it and slide it on the wall until the wire catches the hooks again.

When I turn around the green person is gone.

I grab the envelope, spin around and almost sprint out of the office locking and pulling the door closed behind me.

I take about six strides and run totally smack into one of the office partitions across the hall from Tom's office. I'm stunned and dazed.

"Stop! Robert, you're going to kill yourself," I say out loud, the sound of my own voice frightens me.

I fall back against the cubical wall and begin to take long, slow, deep breaths.

With Tom James' help, will I be able to untie Gordian's knot? I march out of the copy department in dead silence.

I finally get back to my hotel room slump into a chair and try to calm down.

I've got to let Detective Breen know what I've found.

I dial the phone.

"Hello," comes the voice from the phone.

"Mrs. Breen, I'm sorry to call so late, this is Robert Randall, is Detective Breen there?"

"Yes, he is. Frank, its Robert Randall for you."

"Hi, Robert, what can I do for you?"

"I found something that I think you should see."

"Oh, what's that?"

"A white envelope."

"What's in it?"

"I don't know I haven't opened it."

"Where did you get it?"

"I found it in Tom James' office, hidden behind a painting."

"Oh, really, what made you look there?"

"I'll tell you when I see you."

"Not the green blob again?"

"Yes, a green human form again, only this time it was Tom James."

"Shouldn't you open the envelope?"

"I think it's best if I bring it to the police station for them to open. I don't want to contaminate any evidence that might be in it."

"Well, it's a little late to meet you now, why don't you meet me in the Detective's Squad Room at the 18th Precinct at eight in the morning? I'm sure the contents of the envelope will keep until then."

Okay, I'll be there."

"Robert, put the envelope into a larger envelope to protect it."

"I will. Goodnight, Detective Breen."

"Goodnight, Robert, see you tomorrow."

Another murder

It's 6:30 a.m. and room service is knocking on the door to deliver my breakfast. The phone rings just as I'm looking forward to sitting down to a bowl of "Wheaties."

"Robert, this is Detective Breen, there's been another murder."

His words reverberate through the axons of my brain, illuminating questions about virtually every aspect of Tom James' murder. For a moment I stare at the telephone receiver.

I get up and go and open the door for room service.

"Your breakfast, sir."

I point to the center of the room, while picking up some cash from the dresser and handing it to the waiter.

"Thank you, sir."

He shuts the door and is gone.

"Robert, did you hear what I said?"

"Who was it?"

"A junior copywriter named Lloyd Campbell."

"Lloyd Campbell? I know him he is the new writer on the General Brands account."

"Do you know any reason why someone would want to kill him?"

"No, he was a really nice guy, everybody liked him."

"Did he have any thing to do with Tom James?"

"Yes, I believe so, Tom had him working on some sort of special project on the General Brands account."

"Do you know what the special problem was?"

"I'm not sure, there are a lot of problems on the General Brands account, they used to work on it alone at night in Tom's office."

"Do you know Lloyd's parents?"

"Yes, I met them when they came in the office, once."

"Do you think you could go and see what you can find out from them? They would probably tell you more than they would tell me."

"Yes, of course, I'd be glad to. Do they know he's dead?"

"They do, and are very upset about it."

"What do you want me to find out?"

"Try to find out what was going on in his life – his friends, enemies, interests – anything out of the ordinary. And, see if they know anything about what he was working on with Tom James."

"How was Lloyd murdered?"

"He was shot last night in the bathroom at the agency. The crime scene team is still there. The lab is checking the bullet with the one we took from Tom James' body, although it might be different, Tom was shot with a rifle."

"Okay, I'll go see his parents right away."

"We'll meet at the 18th Precinct this afternoon to check out that envelope.

"I'll call you to let you know when I'm done."

A visit to Lloyd Campbell's parents

I'm turning around and there is a loud roar, as the bus I just stepped off of zips past my nose. I'm not paying attention to where I'm going, Detective Breen's call still has me reeling. Why was Lloyd Campbell murdered? What, if anything, did his death have to do with Tom James' death? The case has just gotten a lot more complicated. Could it be that Tom wasn't killed by someone who hated him, but for a totally different reason? I cross the street and I'm standing on the sidewalk in front of "Zum Sammtisch," a German restaurant in the Glendale section of Queens, near the Brooklyn line, looking up at the 3rd floor where I believe Lloyd Campbell's parents live. I enter the narrow glass-paneled door next to the restaurant. On the wall in the small foyer is a row of mailboxes with the name "Campbell" on box number "321." I press the button above the number. A buzzer opens the inner door and I begin the climb to the 3rd floor. As I do, the aromas penetrating through the walls wake up my taste buds. I've always liked German food and I can smell the Sauerbraten, a vinegar-flavored pot-roast, cooking in the restaurant kitchen somewhere below. Carl Lecher told me the name of the restaurant means something like "reserved special table for locals," in German. When I exit the staircase onto the 3rd floor, the hallway is painted in a high-gloss yellow ochre with dark brown trim. There are sconces along the walls spreading fans of light up to the elaborately embossed tin ceiling. I press the bell in the center of the olive green door with the number 321 on it. The door slowly opens. A small woman who I recognize as Lloyd's mother, dressed in a colorful housecoat and slippers, appears holding a handkerchief to her nose. She nods acknowledging me, turns and begins shuffling into the apartment, beckoning with her hand for me to follow her. She seems to be in a trance.

"I'm Robert Randall, I worked with your son at DDBO."

"That's nice."

"He was a good person, I'm sorry for your loss, Mrs. Campbell."

"Those sons-a-bitches, they killed him."

She motions for me to sit on the sofa, the clear plastic cover makes a crinkling sound.

"Who killed him, Mrs. Campbell?"

"Those liquor bums."

"Liquor bums?"

"Yeah, they worked him to death."

"You think someone at the General Brands Company is responsible for your son's death."

"Your talking crazy, Irma," says an old man, wearing dark brown pajamas, as he comes into the room.

"You're Mr. Campbell?"

"That's right. What's your name again, young man?"

"I'm Robert Randall, I met you several years ago when I worked with your son at DDBO."

"What do you want with us?"

"The police asked me to come and see if you know anything about your son's death."

"What do you want to know?"

"Has your son seemed different lately? Has he done anything out of the ordinary in the past 6-months?"

"He did start to spend a lot of time with that Tom James guy."

"Do you know what they were working on?"

"Something to do with those booze guys."

"You mean the General Brands account?"

"That's right, but he wouldn't tell us what he was doing. Everything was so secret you'd think he was working with the FBI or something."

"Did he have many friends?"

"Just some of the kids he went to school with who still live in the neighborhood, but he hasn't been seeing any of them lately, he's been too busy."

"Do you know if he had any enemies?"

"Not a one, everybody loved him. He was such a good boy," his mother interjects.

"Did you ever meet Tom James?"

"No, he only talked to our Lloyd on the phone late at night, he wouldn't talk to us."

"How many times would you say he called?"

"Maybe three or four."

"When was the last time?"

"A couple of nights ago."

"Do you have any idea what they talked about?"

"No, we couldn't hear, Lloyd always went into his room and closed the door. Something was fishy about those calls; Lloyd never kept any secrets from us. But look what I found in his room."

She takes a folded piece of paper from the pocket of her housecoat and hands it to me.

"Here, look at this."

When I unfold it it's an application for a pistol permit that he had filled out.

"Do you know of any reason why Lloyd would need a gun?"

"Not my sweet Lloyd, he would never harm a fly."

"It certainly would indicate that he was afraid for his life."

"Our Lloyd was such a good boy."

"Well, thank you Mr. and Mrs. Campbell, I appreciate your taking the time to talk to me. Can I take this application?"

"Yes, who do you think killed our Lloyd?"

"I don't know Mrs. Campbell, the police are working on it. I'll let you know if we find out anything."

"Thank you, Robert, God Bless you."

"I'll let myself out."

When I get to the street, I realize that there may be a definite link between Lloyd and Tom's deaths. But what can it be? I've got to report to Detective Breen right away. He doesn't live far from here in Maspeth. I think I'll drop over to see him.

Finally, Edna's pot roast

It's been some time since I've stood here on Detective Breen's front steps. I ring the bell. In a minute I hear the inner door opening and the front door swings open.

"Robert, what are you doing here?"

"I just left Lloyd Campbell's parents and thought you would like to know what I found out."

"Good, come in, we're just about to sit down to dinner."

"Oh, I'm sorry, I can come back later."

"Don't be silly, I'm sure Edna will be glad to have you join us."

My mouth starts to water, at last, after all these years, I'm going to get a chance to taste Edna's cooking.

I follow Detective Breen up the stairs and into the kitchen.

"Robert, it's so good to see you."

"It's good to see you again, Mrs. Breen."

"Robert, please sit down here, right next to me."

"Thank you, Mrs. Breen."

"Please, Robert, call me Edna."

Positioned majestically in the center of the table is a huge platter with a mountain of steaming pot roast stacked on it, surrounded by a perfectly browned necklace of onions. Next to it is the largest gravy boat I've ever seen. My mouth continues to water.

"Here's a plate, Robert, help yourself."

"What did you find out at the Campbell's, Robert?"

"Apparently, Lloyd was working with Tom James on some sort of secret project, related to General Brands. He would get phone calls from Tom James in the middle of the night. The last one was just days before the both of them were killed."

"Did his parents know what the calls were about?"

"No, but they both believe that the General Brands people are responsible for their son's death."

I dig into the mound of pot roast and heap as much as my fork will carry onto my plate, carefully spearing a few onions in the process.

"They're more upset about how hard they made him work. And they found this in his desk."

I take the pistol permit application from my pocket and hand it to him, only pausing for a few seconds in my quest to load my plate with pot roast.

"What is it?"

"An application for a pistol permit."

"A what?"

"Apparently he was going to apply for a pistol permit. According to the date on it he had only filled it out the day before he was killed."

"That puts a whole new light on this case."

I delicately glide the gravy boat over my plate and release it like hot lava all over the succulent meat. The aroma has an immediate effect on my taste buds and I begin to salivate more profusely.

"Robert, is there any way you can find out what Lloyd and Tom James were working on?"

I temporarily ignore him and cut a piece of pot roast, bathe it in

Edna's rich, thick, dark gravy and lift it to my mouth with a slice of onion, Mmmm, at last.

"I'll...mmm...check into that tomorrow, Frank."

"Robert, here are some egg noodles."

"She made those noodles fresh this morning, Robert," Detective Breen asserts, with a twinkle of pride in his eye. "Try them with the gravy."

I settle in for some serious eating, only nodding and smiling at detective Breen's comments for the rest of the meal. I've got to call the desk sergeant at the 13th Precinct and let him know even though I didn't get to try Edna's corned beef I did get a taste of her pot roast and egg noodles. He'll probably be jealous.

"Frank, here's the envelope I found in Tom's office."

"Good, I'll bring it in to the 18th Precinct tomorrow to be examined. Meet me there."

"I'll let you know when I'll be there."

A possible motive

I go back to the hotel.

When I open the door to my room I hear the phone ringing.

"Hello, Robert, this is Bill Gunther in the New York office," the voice on the other end declares.

"Yes Bill, how are you?" It's been a long time.

Sven told me you are working with the police on Tom James' murder."

"That's right."

"I'm going down to the printer to do a press check on the General Brands pricelist cover and there's someone there I want you to meet, I think he may be able to fill you in on a few things about General Brands that might relate to Tom's death."

"Okay, what time are you going?"

"Around ten."

"I'll meet you in front of the office at 10 a.m.

"Good, I'll be there."

The temperature in the City is still steamy as I hustle down Madison Avenue.

"Hi Bob." Bill greets me in front of the agency building.

"Hi, Bill, it's good to see you again."

Bill is the production man assigned to the General Brands account.

He's an old-timer and has been at DDBO for eons. He has a slight build, wavy white hair, fine wire rimmed glasses and a pleasant smile. I used to work with him on the account.

"I was scheduled to go to the printer today to check the proof of the cover of the General Brands price list."

"Who's the printer?"

"Acme Printing they do all the printing for General Brands. This price list is a huge job for them – they're printing over 20-million of them – so they want to make sure the cover is just right. It goes to every liquor store in the country. The client wants me to sign-off on it before they turn on the presses. And as I mentioned, there's a man down there that I think you should meet."

"Great, let's go."

Bill raises his arm and a cab cuts across two lanes of traffic and comes screeching to a stop at the curb in front of us.

"Hop in, Bob."

"Where to?"

"114 Varrick Street."

The driver flips down the flag and we're off.

"Who picked the printer?"

"Are you kidding? The client, who else?"

"That cuts out the commission for the agency."

"That's right, they don't want anybody getting any "bene's" except General Brands."

I know they have a reputation for controlling everything.

"The ad manager, Larry Ryan, is a son-of-a-bitch. He wants everyone and everything under his thumb. It's the culture of the client, the rumor is that they are still a bunch of gangsters," Bill adds.

"I know Larry Ryan, remember I worked with him when I was the art director on the account years ago? He is a son-of-a-bitch."

After 20 blocks, the cab pulls up to 114 Varrick Street.

"Time to check the proof and maybe find out a few things."

We head into the building and down a long dimly lit hallway. Our feet begin to feel the vibrations from the huge offset presses running in the basement below. Suddenly we enter a large reception room at the end of the hall.

"Hello Mr. Gunther."

"Hello Janet, we're here to see John Gleason."

"I'll get him for you."

She picks up the phone, "Mr. Gleason? Mr. Gunther is here to see you."

"Please sit down gentlemen, Mr. Gleason will be right up to see you."

Now we can more vividly hear the endlessly repetitious sounds of the presses whirring from the spiral staircase behind the receptionist. "Row, row, row…"

"Hi, Bill." John Gleason's head appears at the top of the staircase. He is a heavy-set man of about 45 with deep-set eyes and dark curly hair. He looks Italian.

"Hello, John, this is Bob Randall he's the creative director in the Boston office. I thought he should meet you. He's working with the police on the Tom James murder case."

"He is?"

"Yes, they asked him to assist a Detective Breen with the case, Bob had worked with him on his great uncle's murder case when he was in art school, years ago."

"That's very interesting."

"Bob has some questions about General Brands, and I thought there's no one who knows more about the General Brands people than you do."

"Let's get the press check out of the way first and then we can go to lunch and talk about General Brands. Follow me gentlemen."

We move behind John down the wide spiral staircase to the pressroom below. As we make the second turn around the great staircase the gigantic pressroom comes into full view. It's breathtaking. The space is cavernous, two football fields wide and six football fields long. There are a dozen 8-color lithographic offset presses strung end-to-end filling the entire room. John motions for us to follow him to a press at the back of the room, a Web Offset press, which means the job is printed on one continuous roll of paper, like a newspaper. Next to the press is a light table with controlled lighting to simulate daylight, where I can see a proof of the catalog cover resting. The job is being run 4-up, which means four price lists are being printed at one time. At the end of the press run the sheet is folded, saddle stitched and trimmed to size as a finished price list. Saddle stitched means the pages are spread over a stainless steel saddle and stapled together from the bottom. They are then packed in boxes and shipped to the liquor stores all around the country, region by region. At the moment the press is silent, waiting for the proof check, so it can spring back into action.

"Here we are, Bob, as long as you are here we might as well get your professional opinion, how does it look to you?" Bill invites me to review the proof.

I take the small magnifying loupe that I always carry from my pocket to check the dot pattern of the color separations on the fresh proof sitting on the light table. The four colors, magenta, cyan, yellow and black, that are used to make up the photos, form a symmetrical star-like pattern when they are in perfect registration. I take a look.

"The registration looks good. Do you have the original transparency?"

"Right here," John hands it to me.

I put the transparency up on the light box.

"Looks like the color halftone needs some minor tweaking. I'll circle the areas that need correction."

I mark pluses and minuses of the various changes in color required. I put a "+R" on the flower to tell them add red, "a -Y" on the liquor in the glass to remove yellow, and, a "+K" on the bottle to add black to the detail. "K" stands for "Key Plate," referring to the black plate.

"John, these should do it."

"Robert, I'm glad you're here to check out this cover."

John takes the proof with my marks and shows it to the pressman, who makes minor adjustments to the appropriate ink fountainheads to increase and decrease the appropriate colors. The pressman then lifts the plastic safety cover over the main power switch and presses the red start button and a loud warning horn sounds, "bwoop, bwoop…" The press slowly begins to turn picking up speed like a subway train, with almost the same sound. Within a minute it's at full speed and the paper is spinning around the plate cylinders popping flat proof sheets onto the skid at the end of the press. "Swish, swish…"

After a few minutes the pressman reaches for the black stop button and presses it. The press slowly comes to a stop. He pulls a sheet off the top of the pile and floats it onto the light table. I step up and closely examine the proof, comparing it to the previous one I had marked. "Perfect, John. Okay to go."

"You know the routine, just sign and date the proof at the bottom, please Bob."

"I think I'll let Bill do the honors, he's the official in charge."

"Absolutely, thanks for a great job, John."

"Now let's get some lunch?"

"Sure."

"If you gentlemen will wait up in the reception room, I'll clean up and be up there shortly."

Within minutes John appears.

"How would you men like to go to Luchow's?"

"The German restaurant on 14th Street?"

"Yes, it has great food," Bill confirms.

"Sounds good to me. Let's go."

When we arrive at Luchow's the host recognizes John Gleason immediately, "John, nice to see you again. Your usual table?"

The restaurant has an old European charm with high walnut panel ceilings and walnut panels on all the walls. There are classic linen tablecloths on all the tables with tall crystal glasses and ornate silverware precisely lined up on either side of a large elegantly gold-leafed plate. Romantic music is permeating throughout the air of this gigantic dining room emanating from a strolling violinist playing the classic German love song, Lili Marleen. The host directs us to a huge booth against the far wall, we settle in and order drinks. I have my usual milk, which generates a few looks from surrounding tables.

"John, I'm glad to have the chance to talk to you about our mutual client, General Brands. Do you know much about their history?

"I know some, what to you want to know?"

"John, from what I understand, this company started during prohibition smuggling liquor into the United States and distributing it underground throughout the country."

"That's right, they're gangsters."

"Gangsters?" I can't believe it.

"Bad people."

"Really?"

"As you said Bob, most of the big liquor companies were started by bootleggers and smugglers during prohibition."

"Yes."

"Back in those days there was out-and-out war going on between rival gangs."

"Were they killing each other?"

"Absolutely. To avoid the local authorities, most of the contraband was brought into the country over the ocean into the remotest beaches of northern Maine. The gangs would try to intercept each other's cargos as they were being lugged over the rocks and jetties onto the beach. People would die in the fights that ensued."

"That sounds a little scary."

"They've cleaned up their acts quite a bit, but there is still bad blood, to this day, between the surviving companies. Today, the General Brands is run by a gangster."

"I have heard that he's a tough guy named Salvatore Vanucci, and that he was a bootlegger in the 20's and that's how he started the company."

"Do you know of any illegal things that they are still doing?"

"Well, I think you may want to tread lightly there. You are better off not knowing too much. By the way, I recommend the "Steak Tar-Tar," it's superb."

"Seriously, are they still using strong arm tactics to force the bartenders to use their brands?"

"There are some who say they are."

"What do you think?"

"You didn't hear it from me, but I have been told that some bartenders have disappeared after refusing to stock the General Brands."

"Have the police looked into it?"

"The local police seem to look the other way when it comes to General Brands."

"You mean they are being paid not to find anything?"

"They don't even look."

"When was the last time this happened?"

"About a year ago."

"Where?"

"In Queens."

"What bar was involved?"

"A place called "Zum Sammtisch," a German restaurant and bar in Glendale, Queens."

"I know that place, I've been there."

"You have?"

"Yes, that just might be the link to Tom James' murder."

"Really?"

Another DDBO person, who was also murdered, lived over the Zum Sammtisch restaurant."

"That's unbelievable."

"Do you know if anything has happened here at Luchow's? This is a German restaurant also."

"Not that I know of. And I think I would have heard, I'm in here all the time."

"Thanks, John, I appreciate your sharing that information with me."

"Be careful, Bob, these are rough people you are dealing with."

"You be careful, too, John."

"Don't worry I will."

"It's just possible Tom James' obnoxious personality got him in too deep with these people."

"Bob, I don't think these people take any guff from anyone."

"Thanks John, Bill, I'm going to run along now, thanks for all your help"

After lunch, I leave a message for detective Breen at the Precinct to let him know I'm heading over to meet him.

Now for the conclusion, hold onto your hats

I've never been inside the 18th Precinct. It's located on west 54th Street in mid-town Manhattan, where most of the action is in the City. The precinct includes some of the most visited tourist sites, The Diamond District, St. Patrick's Cathedral, the Theatre District, Restaurant Row, Radio City Music Hall, and Rockefeller Plaza. The west side of the command is comprised of a residential area.

"Can you tell me where I can find the Detective's Squad Room?"

"Up those stairs over there, down the hall to the back, on the left side." The desk sergeant says, pointing to the staircase.

"Thanks."

"Who are you looking for?"

"Detective Breen."

"He retired years ago."

"I know, he's meeting me here."

"Okay."

As I enter the squad room, Detective Breen is standing by a desk with the envelope I had given him in his hands. He's wearing white gloves.

"You are not going to believe what's inside this envelope you found."

"What is it?"

"It's the answer to the whole case."

He slowly slides a photo and a sheet of yellow copywriter's paper out of the envelope and turns the photo toward my face.

I can't believe what I am seeing.

"Bob, it's a communication from Tom James from beyond the grave."

I'd know his distinct yellow copy paper anywhere. It's a special higher quality bond paper and it's a pale yellow color. Tom's typewriter is also distinct; it's the smaller size "elite" style font. There are two different size typewriter fonts the smaller one is elite and the larger one is pica. When I am deciding what typeface to use in an ad, I have to convert the typewritten copy to the actual typeface in the ad. I have to count every individual character. In the case of Tom's typewriter the "c" and "s" characters are miss positioned above the line.

I recognize the person in the old photo immediately, it's Larry Ryan, the General Brands client, and he's in a Nazi uniform sporting a large, bright red swastika armband.

"Frank, what is this all about?"

"This note from Tom James answers it all. It says: 'If anything happens to me Larry Ryan of General Brands is responsible,' and its signed Tom James."

"Wow."

"God only knows where Tom James got the picture of Larry Ryan in a Nazi uniform."

"This is unbelievable, what does Larry Ryan have to do with Tom James' death."

"Come with me, I want you to meet someone."

"Who?"

"You'll see, I think you'll be surprised."

Frank leads me down the hall to what appears to be a small detention room. As he swings the door open I can't believe my eyes. Sitting behind a small table in the center of the room is Al Lindsay, the old copywriter who spent his life working and drinking on the General Brands account.

"Al, what a surprise to see you. I thought you retired."

It's good to see you, Robert, how have you been?"

"I'm still drinking milk. What are you dong here Al?"

"It's a long story."

"What do you know about Tom James' death?"

"It all began when I overheard a conversation at General Brands. I was waiting in the reception room to see Larry Ryan. I told the receptionist I had to use the restroom. When I proceeded down the corridor I went past the conference room and the door was open a crack. I could barely see in, but I could hear voices. Naturally I stopped and listened.

"He's going to tell the world, we've got to kill him," the rotund man standing at the head of the conference table bellowed as he pounded his fist on the table, rattling the glasses and water pitcher on the metal tray in the center of the table. I recognized the man as Salvatore Vanucci, the Chairman of the Board of General Brands. Over the years I had been in a few meetings with him.

"He's only bluffing," the smaller man sitting at the side of the table responded. I couldn't see who he was."

"Bullshit, he's going to expose us all, we've got to get rid of him before he does."

"What makes you so sure he even knows anything about us?"

"I'm certain that he saw a note on my desk when he was here for the Saint Petersburg Vodka meeting."

"How could you let that happen?"

"I didn't. During the presentation, he needed a piece of paper to block out some words on a layout to make a point. He went to my desk and picked up the note from Barry Cohn about the next meeting of the group, which was lying face down on the stack of papers in my in-box."

"What did it say?"

"It said, 'The next meeting is set for Friday, March 10th at 8:30 p.m. at Zum Sammtisch. ' "

"That doesn't mean anything. It could be a meeting for any one of the brands."

"But, Barry signed it 'Heil Hitler' with a big swastika."

"That could have just been a joke."

"We can't take a chance. He might even know about our master plan."

"What are we going to do?"

"We must kill him."

"But how are we going to do it?"

"We've got to get one of our people to do it."

"Who exactly, who can we trust?"

"Someone we own, someone who owes his life to us."

"But will he do it?"

"He'll do it or we'll have him killed."

"Are you sure this will keep our secret, suppose he has told someone about us?"

"We have no choice, we have to silence him, now."

"Al, you never told the authorities about what you heard?"

"No, I was scared to death, I wasn't sure who they were talking about, but I realized that I had just heard something that could get me into a lot of trouble. Even get me killed. I rushed back to the reception room and proceeded to act as normally as I could. After the meeting with Larry Ryan I went straight back to the office and never told a soul. I was afraid for my life. When Tom James was killed I decided to tell the police what I heard. It was then I realized that Vanucci was talking about Tom James."

"Frank, this is unbelievable."

"They got Larry Ryan to kill them both."

"Both?" Al questions.

"Yes, he shot Lloyd Campbell, also. We think Lloyd saw him in a Nazi uniform going in or out of the basement of the Zum Sammtisch restaurant where the group held their meetings. Lloyd lived right upstairs, over the restaurant.

"That must be why Lloyd was going to buy a gun."

"Yes, and they also murdered one of the bartenders at the Zum Sammtisch who probably found out about the group," I add.

"How did you find out about the murder of the bartender?"

"From a man who has done business with General Brands for many years. He thought the bartender was killed because he wouldn't serve General Brands liquor. He is convinced that the General Brands people are gangsters."

"That's not the half of it, just before you walked in I got a call from Agent Kyle Sheppard of the Secret Service, it seems they have been tracking the Nazi group for weeks. Apparently they were plotting to assassinate the President of the United States because he was pushing for the new legislation to dramatically increase the Federal tax on the liquor industry. It was going to cut sales and cost the liquor industry millions." Frank says.

"How did Tom James fit into the picture?"

"According to Agent Sheppard, Tom James called them on the day he was shot and told them about a note he had seen in the meeting he attended at General Brands. He wasn't sure what it was about but he was suspicious of the signature."

"Tom must have gotten the photo of Larry Ryan from Lloyd."

"That makes sense."

"Well Frank, it turns out that Tom James is not such a bad guy after all, he may even be a national hero. I'm going to have to totally change my opinion of him. I can't wait to tell his wife Hilda. Everyone at DDBO is going to flip over this."

"The Secret Service has already rounded up the entire Nazi gang including Ryan and Vanucci. Our case is solved."

"And I can finally get back to Boston. Although, I must say, living-it-up at the Regal Hotel has been fun."

CPSIA information can be obtained
at www.ICGtesting.com
Printed in the USA
BVHW050954070323
659875BV00017B/114